ANY MAN
A Fictionalized Account of a
Mysterious Disappearance

Louise Corum

ANY MAN

A Fictionalized Account of a
Mysterious Disappearance

Louise Corum

Reverberator Books

For Jeanette.

Published by Reverberator Books.

Paperback ISBN-13: 978-0-9837050-4-8
Paperback ISBN-10: 0-9837050-4-6

First published in the United States and United Kingdom in 2005 by The Book Factory under the title *Any Man: A Fictionalized Account of Something That Really Happened.*

eBook ISBN–13: 978-0-9837050-5-5
eBook ISBN–10: 0-9837050-5-4

Prologue

From what I gather, this is what happened. The story has been in my family for many years and I've managed to piece together bits of information here and there. But none of the information ever made much sense. It happened so long ago most everyone has forgotten about it and they never talk about it. It came to me through my mother who had been told about it by my grandmother. She told me the story of my father's sister who disappeared.

"What happened?" I'd ask her over and over.

"She just disappeared one day," she'd tell me every single time. "No one knows what happened to her. She was supposed to come home on the train but she never got there. Your grandfather looked everywhere for her. He never gave up looking."

That's all she knew, leaving me wondering exactly what happened to her, to the missing sister. It was a story I wanted to understand, a mystery I wanted to solve. But without anything to go on, I was forced to come to my own conclusions about what happened.

So that's what I did. My conclusions are as follows—fictionalized, of course.

This Is What Happened

At the foot of the Cumberland Appalachian Mountains sits a little town appropriately called Cumberland Gap, or, as the locals call it, "the Gap." It's an eastern Tennessee town which borders Kentucky and Virginia. If you hiked up to the Pinnacle, which is a little clearing that sits atop the mountain, you could see all three states at once. To most everyone that does that, it just looks like a bunch of trees. Breathtaking, but trees nonetheless.

The town's main claim to fame is that Daniel Boone blazed a trail through there. There is also a skiffle song called *Cumberland Gap*. In addition to that, during the Civil War, the Confederates hid in the Gap and waited on the approaching Union soldiers. The day that battle was fought was a win for the Confederate side. But they still went on to lose the war.

That's about it. Not much happens in Cumberland Gap. It is a typical southern town that was settled long ago by the Scots-Irish, the English and the Welsh. And, of course, it has always been occupied by the Cherokee Nation of American Indians.

Back in the early 1950s, it looked about the same way as it does now. Lawson's Grocery, which sat on the corner, has long been gone but the post office is still where it sat years ago. The old houses still sit along the picturesque street and the road which leads out of the town and into a little settlement called Tiprell is still there.

Taking that road, you would drive about a quarter of a mile and come upon my grandparent's former home, a small A-frame house that used to be my grandmother's pride and joy. The house once sat on about twenty acres of woodland but has long since been broken up and sold off. The house, which was once well-kept and cleaned fastidiously by my grandmother, is now in disrepair and no longer visited by members of the Muroc family. Inside that house, secrets still reside, secrets that have long been forgotten by the ones who carried them and are now forever out of reach for the ones who follow.

Time does not stand still for anyone but it seems to pause in the old, abandoned house where my grandparents raised their children. There is a sense of nostalgia and longing that permeates it. It's just an ordinary old house but there's something special about it. Something about it seeks redemption. It makes a person want to step inside and look for clues. Or maybe reassure it that its family will be back someday. But they won't come back, just as there aren't any clues in that old house. Just as the walls don't talk, though if they could, would they help unlock the secrets? Would they tell stories? There were good and bad times, as there are in anyone's home. Maybe it longs to mention the children that ran in and out of the old screen door that always creaked when opened. Would the walls tell us the biggest secret of all—what happened to my aunt, Ella Muroc? Do the walls have any idea of what happened? No, and no one else did either.

No one knew, of course, what had happened and that kept them from talking about it. It wasn't a family secret; in fact, it wasn't a secret at all. It was just something no one ever talked about. No one ever said anything about it. Just like no one ever spoke of Ella, my aunt who went missing.

From what I've been told, Ella was a very pretty young woman. She had a lovely heart-shaped face and full red lips along with dark hair. But Ella wasn't just pretty, she was kind, too. She helped my grandmother raise her four younger siblings. Never one to complain, she would instead offer her services up with a smile.

Ella was the oldest of five children. She was the second born, though. The first born, a boy named Edward, died when Ella was a baby. He'd fallen off the bed and onto his head. My grandparents were sick with grief and my grandmother, Ruth, swore off having any more children. Ella was almost eight years old before her sister Susie came along. After Susie, Ruth got back into the groove to give birth two more times. She had another girl, Irene, and the twins, Ray and Roy. At five children, she told her husband she was finished. She would sometimes say if she hadn't had Ella around to help her, she didn't know what she would have done.

Ella was a joy in my grandparents' lives, a joy to behold, a joy to be around. Unassuming, she was easy on the eye and soft on the emotion. My grandparents had big plans for Ella and even saved money to send her to college. Because she'd worked so hard to help her parents out, they believed she deserved something for her efforts. There were big plans for Ella until Harry Thompson.

Harry was a kid down the road, younger than Ella. He was seventeen and she was eighteen and things are just bound to happen. She was saving money and had plans to leave home the next year to attend college. She'd put off college long enough, mostly because her mother didn't want her leave home. However, she knew it was about time. But Harry stopped her in her tracks.

My grandfather's name was William Muroc, but people always called him Doc. He grew up in a tar-papered shack on the side of the Cumberland Mountain with no running water and cracks in the floorboards that were big enough to slide a shovel through. When it got cold in the winter, it got *cold* in that house, but when it got hot, it stayed cool.

He grew up as most boys in that area, poor and dreaming of the day he could leave home and start a life of his own. He wanted money too. Money to go to the movies or have a fountain soda. He wanted the same things everyone else wanted during that time, but mostly he wanted to survive his childhood and get on with his life.

Doc's parents disciplined him and his siblings under the strict Baptist religion. They had met and married within a week. They also produced eleven children in eleven years. Doc was the eldest and grew up taking care of his younger siblings. He grew up hoeing tobacco, pulling weeds, cutting hay and milking cows. Sometimes, especially during the winter, he would go to bed hungry. It didn't bother him too much, but he wished for the day when he could have all the food he wanted.

He wasn't encouraged, as most young people weren't during those days, to further his education. He quit school in the eighth grade, taking a job along side his father in the coal mines of Kentucky. The drives to the mines were long and bumpy. He'd climb into the back of an old wagon and sit with the other miners and talk about hunting, fishing and women, probably in that order. He was just a young man. No more. No less. Life was life. And life was hard. No one could change that.

He might have been more than a coal miner had he been given the proper tools to work with or the right path to walk on. He might have made more money, been more important. He could have been a lawyer. Maybe a doctor. But he wasn't. He couldn't be something he had no concept of. He could sign his name, he could read on an eighth-grade level, as that's where his education ended, and he could balance the checkbook. All he was capable of doing is what he did. He didn't have much money and probably never would. But he did have food and shelter and that was good enough. "Enough" and "plenty" were two words he understood and he lived by.

His dream was to have a house and a family to put in it. All he wanted was the ability to work hard to obtain his goal. It wasn't too long before he met the girl he would eventually marry that would give him his family. She came from a large family herself and when she laid eyes on him—and he on her—they both knew they'd be together. They both saw a reason to leave their families and start one of their own. After a short courtship, they walked side by side, if not hand in hand, to the courthouse where they were pronounced man and wife.

They moved into a rented house immediately. It was very small, very old and just about falling apart. As Doc would fix the leaky roof or patch a hole in the floor, he would envision the day when that house, or perhaps a better one, would belong to him and Ruth and the children.

In time and with money saved, Doc bought twenty acres of land and, with help from his brothers and father, built a house. It was a small house but had "real" bedrooms for the kids, a big kitchen and a good-sized living room. He even installed a bathroom, which was the talk of the town. No one had indoor plumbing in those days. Doc was proud of the fact that he was able to provide his family with some of the first.

While he could provide modestly for his growing family, there were no extras, especially since he had taken out a loan to build the house. In time, the house would be paid for but until then, times would be lean. Doc worked every day he could to get that loan paid off. It took years and once he did, he took out another loan, for an old Ford truck so he could occasionally drive Ruth over the mountain to Middlesboro, Kentucky for shopping.

During the day, Doc slept. At night, he would jump onto the back of an International pick-up, which was owned by his neighbor, Clyde Owens, and together, with six to eight men from the area, they would climb the mountain to their jobs, to the mines. The coal mines in those days were very unsafe. The working conditions injured many men. Doc himself had had several injuries and once got stuck inside the mines after a small avalanche. He didn't mind. He sat there for several hours and napped. Immediate danger was never a concern to him but, then again, he didn't believe in danger. He knew it came with the job and, since he needed the job, there was no reason to have any fear about it. If something happened, then it would happen. Until it did, there was nothing anyone could do about it.

No one complained about the conditions in the mines, they were taken as part of the job. The black spit the lungs produced from the coal dust was overlooked. It was part of the job. It didn't take long for the job to take its toll on Doc's body, especially his knees, which were always black and blue and sometimes bled. He would have to sit on them day in and day out in order to work down deep in the earth, in order for him to chip away at the coal embedded in the mine walls. He didn't let it bother him, though, and never really complained about the pain. He did walk stooped, somewhat, to alleviate the pain which dwelled in his knees and back. But whenever he felt the pain, he'd take a chew of tobacco and that would help take his mind off it.

With his pay, he could not spoil his family, but he was able to provide for them. His children never went hungry as he had. And each year at the beginning of school, each child was given a new pair of shoes and a new set of clothes. Doc was very proud of himself. He liked to see his girls in the cotton dresses with their hair done up in pigtails. He liked to see his boys racing home from the two-room schoolhouse for lunch. Doc always made sure to get up from bed to eat lunch with his family, as he was never able to make it for supper.

Most weeks, Doc worked six days. Those were long weeks, but he didn't mind. He was doing what a man should—providing for his family. He was happy to do so. That's what was expected of him and on Sunday he rested while the family went to church. He never went himself, as he grew up in church and thought he had learned everything he needed to know about God, Jesus and the Holy Ghost. Besides that, he didn't trust preachers. Also, it interfered with his hobby, fishing.

On Sundays, as soon as the family set off to church, Doc went out to the little shack behind the house and grabbed his rod and reel. He would walk alone to the bank of the river, a half-mile away. There he'd sit, watching the river burble and hope for a big catch. Mostly, though, he napped. Sometimes another fisherman or two would come by and disrupt him and his calm. Mostly, it was just him, the water and the fish. He'd whiled many a morning and afternoon away on that river bank.

Life was good to Doc because what he put into it, he got back.

Time moves quickly when you have a young family. Soon, the girls were growing and growing quickly. It embarrassed Doc to see them mature. He had always thought of them as babies. It bothered Doc when he was awakened during the middle of the afternoon by some boy who would call over the fence to them. It also angered him and a few times, he jumped out of bed and ran the boys off.

Doc had good girls. Ella, Irene and Susie were very devoted daughters who loved him more than anything. They were beautiful, so beautiful in fact, that Doc couldn't believe they came from him. Of course, he thought of his wife as pretty, but when he looked at his girls, he saw beauty. He had never really considered himself to be handsome but was quite persnickety about his appearance. He never left the house in anything but overalls but those overalls were clean and starched as was his white cotton shirts. The boots on his feet might have been worn down at the heel, but they were polished before he left the house. All of his children were the same way. At first, it amused him to see them taking after him, but then he wondered about who his girls were seeing, or who was seeing them, looking so neat and clean. The thought of some "old boy" getting a hold of one of his girls scared him. Not only that, it scared him to know that they would leave home soon with men of their own and they would start their own families. He knew most of the boys in the county desired his girls. When he first noticed it, he found himself paranoid that something was going to happen to one of them. So, he kept an eye on them and kept them away from the boys by threatening them with beatings, which he never produced. He kept them in line by fear, but that only works for a while.

He wanted more for his children. Each week, from the time Ella was born, Doc saved a few dollars for their education. He would leave the type of education up to them, whether it was college or trade school, but he knew they would do something better than what he had done. He wanted more for them than the life he led.

But girls will be girls.

One day, they all skipped school to go to the river. When Doc found out, he was livid. He didn't punish them himself, he made Ruth do it. Ruth busted their bottoms with a belt and after it was over, Doc went outside and threw up. He cried for a little while, too and vowed that he would never let one of his daughters hurt again.

The twin boys, Roy and Ray, were another story. They were rowdy, rambunctious. Ruth could beat them day in and day out and they'd never change or "straighten up." But Doc enjoyed the way they were. They liked to wait on him in the early morning to come home from work. They'd wait under the dew filled trees, then pounce on him, laughing. The first time it happened, Doc nearly jumped out of his skin, but soon enough, he came to expect it. And even to look forward to it.

Life was good. Life was filled with children, a wife and a job. That's all Doc needed. In fact, he sometimes wondered why anyone would want anything more.

Gone Fishing

From what I've been told, my grandfather was very upset by the fact that Ella had become pregnant. That was something young girls didn't do back then, lest they be condemned to a life as "trash." Unfortunately, Ella was not only condemned by her neighbors, she was also condemned by her father.

One Sunday, Doc had decided to leave the river bank after he caught several big ones in a row. He was anxious to get them home to Ruth so she could fry them. He was very content that afternoon and happy about his catch, happy it hadn't rained.

About a quarter mile from the house, he heard a noise, which turned out to be a giggle. He knew that giggle. It was Ella's giggle. She giggled at anything. She was a short girl, a head shorter than he, just an inch taller than her mother. She looked like his other girls with long, dark hair and bright blue eyes that came from her mother. The creamy skin and freckles came from him.

He turned and stared into the woods that followed the old dirt road all the way to the house. He heard the giggle again. His interest was piqued. What was she doing here?

"Ella?" he called, thinking she and her sisters were picking blackberries, as it was time for them to be in.

All of a sudden, the movement stopped.

"Ella?" he called and stepped into the woods. "You alright, girl?"

"Uh…Daddy?"

"Ella, what are you doing?" He started walking towards her voice.

"Daddy, I'll be home in a little bit!" she cried.

"Ella?" he called, feeling panicky. "What's the matter?"

"Nothing, Daddy, I'll be home soon," she said, then nearly cried, "Just go home and I'll be right there!"

But panic had taken over and his natural father's instinct sprang into action. In no time, he was standing in front of her. It took a moment to sink in. Her hair was all messed up and the top of her old calico dress unbuttoned. He stared at her, then glanced to his left where Harry Thompson stood, looking slightly ashamed and very embarrassed.

Doc didn't say a word but many bad thoughts entered his head. He went after this one: *Get him!* He lunged for Harry Thompson's neck. As he lunged, Ella screamed. He caught Harry and they fell to the ground where Doc proceeded to beat the living daylights out of him.

Ella tried to pull him off, but Doc didn't let up until he had Harry officially beaten. Harry Thompson finally managed to get away. He was a bloody mess but he didn't care as he raced through the woods towards his house. And away from them.

Ella was crying. Doc noticed that her dress was now adjusted and buttoned. He started towards her then, but stopped himself. Ella avoided her father's eyes.

They didn't say one word.

Doc turned and left the woods, picking up his rod and reel and his catch on the way out. Ella came out of the woods, head down. She walked quickly towards the house and away from him. Doc was overcome with emotion— shame, frustration, resentment. Mostly anger. Anger that his eldest daughter would do such a thing. But she was now eighteen and a woman. But she wasn't married. He didn't like the fact that he would soon lose her to some boy like Harry Thompson, either. He didn't want her to end up like that. He'd saved for her education, for the education of all his children so they might have a better life than he and Ruth. He resented the fact that Ella had messed all that up.

All he'd done was gone fishing and look at what had happened.

She continued walking, head down, with the occasionally whimper. Suddenly she turned and cried, "Why'd you have to do that?!"

Before he knew what he was doing, Doc had dropped his catch, his rod and reel and was bent grasping a rock. His father had done this to him many times. He had hated it. He had hated his father when he'd done it, and knew he should refrain, but he couldn't help himself. He threw the rock and it hit Ella's shoulder. She cried out and gave him a pitiful look as she'd never been stuck by him before.

"What are you doing, Daddy?" she asked, almost crying.

Doc picked up another rock. It hit her arm. And another one—her elbow. She cried and screamed and soon was running towards the house, calling for her mother, for God, for anybody, somebody to help her. Doc chased her until they reached the house, and he continued to stone her over and over until she was covered with bruises, the same kind that covered his heart.

When she had disappeared into the house, Doc turned and left, went back to the river and stayed there till morning. He didn't regret what he did; he just didn't know what had come over him.

The regret would come later, though.

Ruth said, "She's pregnant."

Doc was not surprised.

"Harry Thompson wants to marry her."

Doc knew better.

"You shouldn't have done that to her, you shouldn't have rocked her," she said, her tone accusatory. "She ain't no animal. Why did you hit her like that? Huh?"

Doc didn't answer.

"Got this whole house tore up," she said and sat down next to him at the table. "Kids are all scared to death of you."

Doc sighed.

"You could have killed her," she said. "If you'd have hit her in the head, you would have killed her."

Doc looked away from her.

"What are we gonna do?" she asked.

Doc didn't know. All he knew was that he had found some happiness with his children and now that all this had happened, now that it was gone, he wondered if it had just been a dream. He had trouble understanding why Ella wasn't a good girl anymore, why she had acted like trash and gotten herself knocked up. Now she'd never leave their small town. She would end up just like her mother, raising children and praying she could feed them. That is, if she could find a man now, which he doubted she could.

He had always looked forward to seeing the kids when he came home from the mines but now it was different, it'd all changed. They were frightened of him, of his actions. There was too much tension and sometimes he'd work over just to avoid going home. The only joy that he'd had was his children. They were his pride and now his pride had been shattered.

"Huh?" Ruth asked. "What are we gonna do?"

He didn't know what to do. He'd leave that up to her mother but he did offer a suggestion.

Ruth gasped. "Are you crazy?"

"What else we gonna do?" he asked. "You want her to marry that old boy?"

Ruth didn't. She knew she had to make a decision and it was the hardest she'd ever made. But she told Doc, "I won't send her if she doesn't want to go."

"She ain't got much choice," he told her.

He was right. So, after the dust settled, there was nothing to do but send Ella to a home for unwed mothers and hope no one in their small community found out.

Of course, the neighbors knew and Ella had to endure prying eyes and whispers. Her once-happy disposition turned sour. Not only had she been forbidden to marry the young man who had fathered her child, she was going to be forced to give her baby away. Her ambitions slowly dissolved and she became a shell of her former self. She was confused and angry that this had happened to her and she wondered why life had to be so hard.

Times were tough for Ella. As Doc's world collapsed, so did hers. No longer did she have a loving father who thought she could do no wrong, to him she was "ruined." No man would want her after he found out she had a child. In the late 1940s, this was the worst thing that could happen to a young girl, especially a young girl who lived in a town the size of Cumberland Gap. After all, her future relied on her virtue. All because she had let that old boy talk her into doing it. How she wished she'd never laid eyes on Harry Thompson.

But without much choice, Ella left home the following week. She was to be taken by train to Knoxville. There she was to stay in a girls' home where she would carry the baby for a while, then she would give birth, sign a paper and give it away to a caring family.

"Mommy," she cried just before she left. "They'll make sure to give my baby to a good family who won't hurt it, won't they?"

Ruth didn't know. She sure hoped so. She smiled through her own tears and nodded. Ella cried. Irene and Susie cried. The twins kept to themselves outside but they cried too.

Ella looked over at Doc who was sitting away from them. She knew his hurt and why he had stoned her. She knew she had fallen in his eyes and might not ever get back to her original standing. She hated that about as much as giving the baby she carried inside her away.

"Daddy?" she called.

Doc ignored her and got up and went outside, where he picked up her cardboard suitcases and started down the road with them. Everyone got up and followed him in silence and they walked all the way into Cumberland Gap and to the train station. Once there, they started crying again.

Doc stood away from the family and knew this was the right thing to do. He looked to the side and saw Harry Thompson standing there, trying to hide himself around the side of the building. Doc felt a flash of anger and cursed under his breath, *Damn him!* He almost ran over to him, as he felt he had some unfinished business, but he stopped himself. Ella's leaving was enough for him to contend with at this moment.

Ella threw him a wounded look before she got on the train. Doc almost crumbled, but his pride was hurt. His pride of knowing his daughter had done such a thing was more than he could bear and his pride refused to let her off the hook.

The train pulled away and Ella was gone. They went back home and Ruth fixed dinner.

Ella stayed in Knoxville for nearly eight months. The baby was born healthy and was given to a family from up north. When Doc found out Ella was coming home in a few days, he began to feel excited. It was all over now, all done. Things had changed, sure, but that didn't mean they couldn't resume their lives. She'd go to school and she'd meet a better boy than Harry Thompson. Things would turn out alright and they could finally put all the bad to rest.

But things had changed and there wasn't anything Doc could do about it. In fact, the lady at the home had asked Ella to stay on. Ella had been a big help and she had offered her a room. Good hands were in short supply and Ella was needed there. She would go to school during the day, help around the home in the afternoon and be paid a small salary, which could go towards her education.

Ella now had a dream. She wanted to be a secretary.

All of this was written in a letter, begging her parents to allow her this chance, this opportunity. She was near the college. She would make a better life for herself.

There was no choice. Ruth and Doc conceded.

A few years passed. Ella came home less and less often. She was growing older, growing up. It was to be expected.

And, as the years passed and Doc watched his children gain maturity, as he watched his wife breathe a sigh of relief, he wondered what came next. He had never allowed himself any fantasies about retiring from the mines, or doing something different. But the idea came to him.

He immediately dismissed it as fancy.

She Wasn't On the Train

It was around the twins' twelfth birthday that Ruth received a letter from Ella.

"Dear Mommy,

I will be coming home by train May 11th, in time for Roy and Ray's birthday. I have bought them a few presents each so you don't have to worry about that. I can't wait to see everyone again! It seems like forever since we've been together. Please tell Irene and Susie that I have bought them a few lipsticks, too. Maybe Daddy will let them wear it finally! I will be at the train depot around 12:00pm. Please meet me there.

Love, Ella.

P.S. Please don't tell Daddy about Frank. I want to tell him myself."

But Ruth had already told Doc about Frank and about how they were going to get married soon. She looked the letter over again and smiled at Doc. She wanted to tell him how crazy Ella was about this man, about how Ella was doing so much better than she'd ever hoped. She wanted to speak, but couldn't find the words.

Doc looked back at her and he knew what she was thinking. She was thinking about how much she missed Ella. She was thinking that Ella's visits would become less frequent, as well as her always cheerful letters. She was thinking about the regret she had of sending her oldest daughter away, for forcing her to give her baby away to strangers. She was thinking about how they could have done things differently, to keep her home with them, to keep her near. But her letter confirmed it. She would never come home to stay. She was almost twenty-three now and a lot of time had passed. She was older, more mature, more beautiful than she'd ever been. She'd graduated from secretary school years ago and secured a good job. She had worked hard to get a small apartment and a life. She was grown up, it was that simple. Ruth's little girl was never coming home to stay. She was sad at this fact, but relieved that she'd done her job by raising her well.

Doc was thinking the same thing.

The house had to be cleaned and the food cooked. Ella must have her favorite, blackberry cobbler. She must have turnip greens and polk salad. She would sleep in the same bed with her sisters, as she always had.

The house was aflutter with activity in anticipation of Ella's arrival. Everyone was excited. They hadn't seen her since Christmas.

Doc was nervous. He had confronted his feelings about Ella's baby and accepted that she had just made a mistake—

no more, no less. He decided he might try to tell her he was sorry. It had been years since he had stoned her but they'd never officially patched things up. It was time to do that. It made him nervous to think about it, let alone talk about it, as he never had. But he knew he should. He wanted to. He wanted her to know he was sorry. Nothing more. Nothing less.

It was a cool day in early May. Blackberry winter was in and though the horizon looked to be warm and inviting, the crisp wind chilled everyone to the bone. Despite the fact that the sun shined, they were dressed in heavy coats that covered up their best clothes, the ones they wore to church on Sunday. Ruth made sure her children looked their best whenever out in public. Doc wore his overalls, though he never went to church, and also donned his newest brown fedora that Ruth had bought for him on her last shopping trip to Middlesboro. The hat came from John's store and was hand-made. Doc was very proud of it and liked the way it fit his head.

It was around noon when the train arrived. As black smoke blew from the smokestack as it rounded the bend, Doc began to smile. He realized he was happy, happier than he had been in a long, long time. It was relief he felt, relief in knowing that the bad times had passed and there was nothing to be hurt or resentful over anymore.

Ruth was smiling, too. As were the other children. This was an exciting day for them. They liked the busy little train depot and the excitement of being among people who traveled. Perhaps they thought about the day when they would be on the train and everyone else would be waiting for them.

Ray was bent tying his shoe. Doc noticed how he had grown. He was a tall boy. Roy seemed slightly shorter, always had. That was the only discernable difference in the two.

The train whistled and came to a slow, grinding halt. Almost instantly, people began to exit the train. There was a torrent of activity that lasted for, maybe, a minute. Again, it seemed exciting.

Irene shouted, "Oh! There she is!"

Doc's smile grew deeper.

Irene ran up and grabbed what she thought was Ella's arm. The young woman jerked it back and glared at her. Irene blushed.

"Oh, I'm sorry," she said and moved away from the young woman. "I thought you were my sister."

The young woman nodded and moved away from her. Susie began to giggle.

"You're so stupid, Irene!" she squealed.

Irene's face hardened and she took at swat at Susie.

"Stop it, girls!" Ruth yelled. "Go find your sister!"

The girls glared at each other then pranced off, pushing and shoving.

Ruth looked around, then at Doc and shrugged.

Doc shrugged back and called, "Go see if she's on the train."

Ruth stared at the train, as if trying to decide if that's what she should do.

"Go on!" Doc hollered. "We ain't got all damn day!"

Ruth seemed to jerk, then she climbed the steps onto the train.

"Daddy," Roy said. "Junior Wallace says he's gonna sell his coon dog. It's a blue-tick."

Doc eyed the boy.

"Yeah," Ray chimed in. "He says it's the best dog around. Treed four coons in one night."

Doc said, "Boys, you ain't got that kind of money for that dog."

"But," Roy said. "We was thinking if you lent us some money on it, then we could pay you back."

Doc looked towards the train. Still, no sign of Ella. He noticed that an attendant was pulling out suitcases from the belly of the train. Doc saw that Ella's two cardboard ones were among them. They were the same ones she had taken with her when she left to have the baby. Ruth had bought them new for her then, but now they were getting a little worn. Doc decided to mention to Ruth that she needed new ones and that they should buy her some for when she came to visit.

"Dad—"

Doc ignored the boy and walked towards the suitcases. He was ready to get the hell out of there, get home and get fed. He had to go into work that nigh and dreaded it so much he pushed the thought of the mines out of his mind.

"Forget it, then!" Ray hollered at him.

Doc threw him a stern look over his shoulder. Ray immediately straightened up and looked at his shoes.

Doc shook his head and reached for Ella's two suitcases. The haggard attendant nodded at him, but didn't say a word.

Doc picked up the suitcases and walked back over to the boys and handed each one. He glanced over at the train again. He could see Ruth through the windows. She was flying, nearly running, through the train car. *What was she doing?*

Doc sighed and took a chew of tobacco out of his pocket, bit a piece off and put the rest back. Ray tapped him on the arm and motioned for the tobacco.

"You ain't gettin' no backer," Doc replied and chewed.

"Shit, Daddy!" Ray said. "I'm almost twelve years old! I can have a chew of backer if I want!"

"Then go get your own," he muttered. "Roy, get your ass on that train and tell them to come on."

Roy trotted off and entered the train.

"Daddy," Ray began. "That dog—"

"No, son."

Ray huffed, but kept quiet.

Susie and Irene skipped up, smiling. Doc eyed them. Susie said, "Can't find her."

"What?" Doc asked.

Irene said, "She ain't here, I guess."

Doc sighed with agitation. "She's here. I got her suitcases, see?"

"Daddy, we looked everywhere," Susie said, then bent and rubbed her foot. "My foot's killing me."

Doc shook his head, feeling somewhat frustrated. Just then, Ruth jumped off the train, followed closely by Roy. They rushed over towards them. That's when Doc knew. He didn't know how he knew, but he knew.

Ruth confirmed it, "She wasn't on the train."

The next few days were absolute hell for the entire family. There was a flurry of activity that kept them up all night. Police reports. Questions asked to all train personal, to train passengers. They all said the same thing, "We didn't see her."

No ticket had been taken from her. The only conclusion they had was this: She had made it to the train station. She had checked her bags. Then, for whatever reason, she hadn't gotten on. Friends from Knoxville had been questioned, her apartment searched. People from her job had been interviewed and they all said the same thing, "We don't know anything."

Doc didn't know either. It nearly killed him, not knowing. Not knowing what happened, when it happened, or why it had happened.

After about a month, people stopped coming by to call to say they were sorry, and went back to their own lives and problems. Doc was glad. It was just as well. He didn't like people in his business.

He couldn't accept it, though. He couldn't accept that Ella was gone and might not ever be coming back. He couldn't accept that the FBI had taken over the case from the local sheriff, which meant it was more serious than he wanted it to be. He could not stand the name the FBI had given her: Missing Person. She wasn't missing. In his heart, she was making him pay for the wrong he'd done to her. He began to believe that. Soon, she'd walk through the front door laughing. She'd tell 'em all it was a joke. Maybe she'd run off and gotten married and was too ashamed or something to call. But he knew that wasn't true. The fact was, he had no idea what had happened to her and that drove him almost insane. He couldn't live like that, not knowing what had happened. So, there was only one thing for him to do. And that thing was to find her.

No One Knew Anything

No one knew anything—no one at the train station, at the police station or at the girls' home, which was Doc's last stop in Knoxville. Doc sometimes wondered if someone was playing a cruel joke on him. He wondered the same thing about Miss Abernathy, who ran the girls' home. He sat in front of her, hat in hands and feet crossed. He sat and wondered why this was happening to him and what he could do about it.

Miss Abernathy was a slight woman. She was around Doc's age, maybe younger, maybe older. Her hair was dark, slightly oily and pulled into a tight bun. Her face had an almost pinched look on it most of the time though she had once been considered quite a beauty.

She and Doc sat in silence. It was a silence that neither of them wanted to be part of. They both wanted the visit over and done with. She'd answered all of his questions. She'd told him what a good girl Ella was, how much they wanted her back safe, too. She went into detail about how much everyone loved her, loved having her around. What a joy she was to the home, how she'd helped the other girls.

Doc suddenly asked, surprising himself, "What did her baby look like?"

Miss Abernathy jerked back at the question, as if she'd never been asked that sort of thing. It took her a moment to construct her answer, then she said slowly, "Well, from what I can remember, she was a large baby, almost eight pounds. Head full of black hair..." She nodded in memory but didn't continue.

"She look like Ella?"

She sighed. "Yes."

"Pretty baby, then?"

She nodded. "Very."

"Who'd you give it to?"

"That's confidential."

Doc sighed. "That mean you won't tell me?"

"Yes."

Miss Abernathy began to wring her hands together. She was quite uncomfortable being around someone like Doc, who didn't say much. He looked rough to her, poor even. Nothing like his daughter who was so pretty and pleasant to be around.

"Well, that's all I wanted to ask you," Doc said, knowing he needed to leave, but not wanting to. This was one more place he could cross off his list. One more place where he had came up with nothing. He stood.

Miss Abernathy stood, too. "It was nice meeting you," she said, extending her hand. "I'm sorry I don't know anything. Ella moved out a long time ago. She did drop by once or twice a month, though. She was always good about helping out."

He nodded. "She kept coming here?"

She nodded. "Yes, she wanted to keep giving back, as she said. She liked helping the other girls. She knows what they go through. She'd talk to them a lot. They love having her around."

Doc held his hand out and gave her hand a hasty shake, then pointed outside. "Mind if I go out there and sit on that bench for a bit?" He nodded out the window where a pretty white wrought-iron bench sat under a larger oak tree.

"Of course not," Miss Abernathy said with a tight smile.

He nodded at her and left the room. She pulled the blinds shut, sat down at her desk and, as soon as she knew he was out of hearing distance, burst into tears.

Doc sat on the bench and stared out at the road in front of it. He realized the road went left or right, up or down, south or north. There were so many directions the road reached towards. All infinite. All never ending. All stretching, teeming with possibilities.

Which one to take?

If Ella had left the girls' home, taken a left…taken a left… Left… Left. Where was left? Left. Oh, left lead towards north. So, if left led towards north, she'd eventually reach the train station that would take her home. If she had taken a right, where did that lead? South. Back into town. When she reached an intersection, which way would she have gone? Would she have stopped to ask directions and if so, where had she wanted to go? If you looked at the road, at all the directions in which it could lead you, which way would you go? And why? Why pick one direction over the other?

There were too many possibilities. And none of them made any sense.

It's going to be so hard finding her, Doc thought and immediately a wave of panic overcame him. He was suddenly nauseous and his heart was pounding. He couldn't breathe or think straight. The panic caught in his throat and choked him. The realization of how big all this was was setting in and it was scaring him. He'd been scared before, but not like this. There was nothing he could do about this fear. It was just there. It would always haunt him.

Doc heard some movement behind him. He straightened up and his body became stiff and rigid once again.

"You Ella's daddy?" a little voice asked.

Doc turned to see a child, about a fifteen-year-old child, a pregnant child. He looked away from her quickly. He said, "I reckon."

Uninvited, she sat down next him and smiled. "I liked Ella a whole bunch."

He nodded.

"Did her mommy come with you?"

"No, she didn't."

"How come?" she asked.

"She's got the other kids to tend to, I reckon."

"Ella's got brothers? How many?"

"Two brothers."

"Any sisters?" she asked.

"Two, I reckon."

She smiled, nodding. "I know that. She told me. I know all about her family."

Doc tried to smile back but he couldn't.

"She told me you always wear overalls and that old hat," she said and eyed him. "Why do you always wear overalls?"

Doc thought about that. He didn't know. It had never occurred to him not to. "I don't know," he muttered, wanting a chew of tobacco. He didn't dare pull it out, though.

She nodded again, smiling softly. "I miss Ella."

Doc felt a lump raise in his throat.

"She was real friendly," she said. "And pretty, too. Lots of times real pretty girls ain't real friendly, but she was, real friendly. And pretty, too."

"Uh huh," he muttered and cleared his throat.

"She gave up her baby, too," she said, staring down at her bulging belly. "But that was a long time ago. She said she named it Olivia."

Doc didn't know that. He didn't know the baby had a name, but of course it did. Why wouldn't it have a name?

"I'm gonna give mine to the same people she gave hers to."

"Oh, that right?"

She nodded, smiling widely at him. "That way, they can be sisters. I mean, if I have a girl."

"You know these people?" he asked.

She shook her head. "All I know is their name is Green and they live way up north, in New York City."

"New York City?" he said. "Is that where Ella's baby is?"

She nodded. "Yeah. She told me they're real nice. That's why we talked because they're interested in my baby. Ella knows them pretty good. They sent her a bunch of pictures of the baby. And she went to see it once or twice. You know, after it stopped taking the milk."

"The milk?"

"Mother's milk," she said.

"Oh," Doc said. "Ella lived with them?"

She nodded, then whispered, "No one is supposed to know, though. We're not supposed to, if you know what I mean. And she told me not to tell anyone. But you're her daddy, so I figure I can tell you."

"She never told us she went up there."

"She wasn't supposed to," she said. "Those Green people told Miss Abernathy that the baby needed the mother's milk, so it wouldn't get sick as much."

Doc's eyes narrowed. "Oh?"

"From what she told me," she continued. "Miss Abernathy worked it out so Ella could go up there and have the baby at their hospital and all that. No one knew. She said everyone here was told she went home to have the baby but she didn't."

Doc nodded, wondering about this secret life his daughter had had.

"No one knows but me," she went on. "I know 'cause we're good friends."

"Ella still go up there?" he asked.

"I don't think so," she said. "She told me she hadn't been in years. Said it got harder and harder to leave the baby and all. She said it wasn't right to do that to the baby, to confuse it like that."

"Huh," he said.

"She still gets pictures," she said. "Pretty little girl."

"Uh huh," he muttered.

"They say she didn't come home on the train," she said. "She didn't, did she?"

"No," Doc said, clearing his throat. "Reckon she went to New York to see the baby instead?"

She shook her head. "No, she was really going home. She told me that and said that as soon as I had my baby, I could come with her. Said her mommy made the best biscuits and gravy in the world."

"When was the last time she went to New York?" he asked.

She thought about it. "It's been years, I think, at least two years. Like I said, she said it got harder and harder to leave."

"So, two years?"

"Two or three, I can't remember."

"Why?" he asked. "Why did they keep sending for her?"

"I dunno," she said. "They liked her a lot and the baby loved her. They thought it was good for the baby to know its real mommy. That's why I might give them my baby. They might let me see it some. I'd like that."

Doc nodded, not knowing what to say.

She stood and stretched, placing her hands on the small of her back. "Well, I better get back inside. It was nice to meet you, Ella's daddy. I hope you find her soon. She always brought all of us lipsticks and stuff when she came. And she always made us laugh. This place needs her. It gets so gloomy sometimes."

He nodded at her and asked, "What was your name?"

"They just call me Josie," she said with a smile and walked away.

Doc found himself wandering the streets around the girls' home. He knew Ella lived somewhere around there. He had seen the return address on the letters she sent, but he couldn't remember which house her apartment was in.

He walked up and down the street, wishing he could remember. He stopped in front of a tall Victorian home that had been converted into small apartments. Ella had described a place like this in her letters. Could this be it?

Just then, the front door opened and an older, fat woman emerged, pushing a small grocery cart. She looked at him from the steps and narrowed her eyes.

"What do you want?" she hissed.

"Nothing," Doc said, clearing his throat. "Just looking for my daughter's apartment."

Her expression immediately changed. "Are you Ella's daddy?"

He nodded.

The woman rushed down the steps, abandoning her cart, and took his hand. "We were wondering what happened. No one's called us!"

"We don't know what happened," he said. "That's why I'm here."

"Huh," she said, then jerked. "Oh! Excuse my manners. I'm Miss Sinclair. I'm the landlady."

"Nice to meet you."

They didn't shake hands.

She smiled and said, "Well, I didn't know what was going on, but you come on in. I'll let you into her apartment and you can tell me what you know."

Doc didn't like nosey people and he knew he wouldn't supply her with the little bit of information he'd learned. That was between him and his family and no one else. But he'd be nice to this lady. He'd have to in order to get inside that apartment.

Miss Sinclair unlocked the front door, saying, "We have a lock on the front door, too. Young ladies can't be too careful, you know? We only rent apartments to young ladies. No men allowed are to live here. But of course, you can come in, I didn't mean that. You're Ella's father so of course *you* can come in."

Doc nodded, feeling uncomfortable going into an all-ladies' home. But that's what he had come for.

"And just let me tell you," Miss Sinclair said. "There was no funny business going on here. No, sirree. The girls have to lock their doors right at ten. No visitors after ten. When I took Ella in, she was told that. And, as far as I know, she never broke the rules, Mr. Muroc."

That was good to know.

"Ella had the downstairs apartment," Miss Sinclair said as they went inside and to the first door on the left. "I live out back, in the small guesthouse. Did you know this old house was used as a hospital during the Civil War? It was. They bandaged and saved many Confederates right here in this very house."

Doc was impressed.

"It's been handed down to me from my family," she said and opened the door, then gestured him inside. "I converted it into apartments to bring in some income. I'm disabled—arthritis. I can't work."

Doc walked into the apartment and immediately felt at ease. He could feel Ella's presence there. He could feel it in the small potted plants on the windowsill and in the cheery light yellow paint on the walls and in the old yet comfortable furniture. He could feel it in the cleanliness she'd picked up from her mother. The entire apartment was sparkling clean.

"She decorated it herself," she told him and walked around the small living room. "I told her to do whatever she wanted, it's her apartment, not mine, I said. She did a wonderful job."

He nodded.

"I'll just let you look around," Miss Sinclair said and went to the door. "I hate to run, but I have to do my shopping today. When I get back, we'll have some lunch and sit down and discuss what we're going to do."

"'What we're going to do?'" Doc asked.

"About finding Ella," she said. "This apartment won't be rented out until I find out where that girl went."

"Where do you think she went?"

"Well," she said, pursing her lips. "She said she was going home, to your house, I mean. And… Well, I know she was. She told me she'd be back late Sunday. In fact, I saw her leaving early that morning."

"You saw her leaving for a fact?"

"Of course," she said. "I get up early every day and have my coffee by the window. I looked out and there she was, carrying her suitcases. I waved to her but she didn't see me, so she didn't wave back."

Doc let the image of her walking with her suitcases sink into his mind. What did this mean? It meant what they had told him: She'd gone to the train station, checked her bags and then, for whatever reason, she hadn't boarded. He knew he was still at square one.

He realized Miss Sinclair didn't know anything, either. No one knew anything. Then he thought of something. "What about this boy she was seeing? You know anything about him?"

"I know he's sick with worry," she said. "Nice boy, good looking boy—you've got no worries there, I can assure you, Mr. Muroc."

"You can call me Doc," Doc said. In fact, he'd prefer it.

"Oh," she said and the stern look disappeared from her face for a moment before returning. "I have his number. You can call him if you like."

Doc just stared at her. "Call him?"

"Why, of course," she said and pointed at a big, black telephone sitting on one of the end tables. "Ella had a phone, we all do now, Mr.—I mean Doc. Just sit down and I'll go get his number for you."

She rushed out the door and Doc stood there for a few minutes looking around, feeling that he shouldn't be there without someone with him. When Miss Sinclair reappeared, she thrust a piece of paper into his hands.

"That's his work number," she said. "Just call and ask for Frank Jones and you two can talk."

"Oh," Doc muttered.

She started to the door, leaving Doc stranded in the middle of the living room floor. She turned back to him and said gently, "Go on now."

Doc didn't use the phone much and didn't really know how. He just sat down on the couch and looked at it.

"Oh, here, let me," Miss Sinclair said and dialed the number. She listened, then said, "Yes, please let me speak to Mr. Frank Jones. I'll hold, yes." She put her hand over the phone. "He's in the *insurance* business, you know. He's quite successful."

Doc nodded.

"Very good looking young man," she continued. "Someone I'd like my own daughter to marry. If I had a daughter, but I don't. I've never been married, Mr. Muroc. I like to think of the girls that live here as my daughters."

Doc just stared at her.

"They're lovely, lovely young women," she said. "Very nice and—Oh, Mr. Jones, this is Miss Sinclair...yes, Ella's landlady. Listen, young man, I have Ella's father here and he'd very much like to talk to you." She paused, listening. "Oh, I don't know. Let me ask him." She put her hand over the phone and said, "Would you mind waiting for a bit? He said he'd like to talk to you in person."

Doc nodded. He wanted to talk to this young man in person, too.

She got back on, "Yes, he's here, at Ella's apartment. Please do and hurry. Goodbye to you, too, Mr. Jones." She hung up and smiled. "He'll be here shortly. You just stay put and I'll be back soon. We'll all three have lunch, how's that?"

Doc nodded.

"Be back soon," Miss Sinclair said at the door before closing it softly.

Now Doc was all alone. He looked around uneasily and wondered what to do. As before, he felt Ella in the room and then heard her laughter, but of course it was just his imagination. He got up off the couch and started to look around. He looked in the small bedroom, eying the single bed which was covered with a light green chenille quilt and lots of fancy pillows at the top.

He shut the door and opened the next one, which was the bathroom. He looked it over good, at the black and white tile that covered it and at the bathmat and fluffy white towels, thinking about what luxury his daughter had lived in. They had an indoor bathroom but nothing like this. Ella had a nice life, he realized and for that he was grateful.

He went into the small kitchen and marveled at the appliances and vowed to get Ruth some as soon as they could afford it. That old wood cookstove constantly needed wood and was always so hot that all the kids had burned themselves on it at one time or another. Ella didn't have much in the refrigerator, just some bologna and cheese.

He shut the refrigerator door and sighed, looking around. He went back into the bedroom and to the closet. He looked through it at her clothes, which were so nice and new. He wished he could have given her those clothes, that he could have put them on her back. But there wasn't much he could do about that either.

At the top of the closet was a small, cloth-covered box. He took it down and inside found some pictures, pictures of a fat baby with black hair. He knew right away that it was Ella's baby. There was even one or two of her holding the baby inside of what looked like a fancy house. That was all he found. All except a business card: "Dean Bellows, Attorney at Law," with a Knoxville address.

He glanced at the card and went back to the pictures. He studied the pictures for a long time, not believing he was looking at his own grandchild. It made him feel odd and he stuffed the pictures back into the box and forgot about them.

He didn't find anything in her closet, so he went to a small desk in the corner. Just some letters she'd gotten from Ruth and the kids and some birthday cards. He shut the drawers on the desk and went to the small nightstand drawer, opened it and saw the gun.

"Ella wants your pistol," Ruth had said about a year ago.

"When did you talk to Ella?" he asked.

"This afternoon," she said. "I was just leaving Lawson's when Melvin came out and told me she was on the phone."

He nodded. Lawson's Grocery was the only place in Tiprell with a phone. Everyone got calls there. Ella called a few times a month and would tell the owner, Melvin Lawson, that she needed to talk to her mother. He'd then send his son to the Muroc's home with a message and Ruth would hurry to the store and wait. Ella would call back within an hour's time.

"I told her she could have it," Ruth said. "So you can give it to her."

"What's she want it for?"

"Protection," she said. "Now I told her she could have it."

"Protection from what?" he asked, thinking about it. Sure, everyone he knew had guns; it was an old frontiersmen tradition. Doc had rarely used the gun, preferring his shotgun over it.

"You know what," she said. "Now she wants it, so give it to her."

"Is somebody bothering her?" he asked.

"No!" she snapped. "Good Lord, why do you never say a word and then when I ask you for something, you can't quit talking? Just give her the damn gun."

Doc sent the gun, along with a box of bullets, in the mail to Ella the next day. Back then, anything could be sent through the mail. They never checked. Within a matter of days, Ella had gotten the gun and sent a letter of thanks to her mother.

Doc sniffed the barrel of the gun. It hadn't been fired in a while. He checked the chamber. One bullet was missing.

"Here, girl," he'd told Ella years ago. "Let me show you how to use it." He'd taken the gun from her and pointed it at a tree. "Cock the hammer back slowly and pull the trigger." He fired, then handed the gun to her. "Hold it tight now."

She held it steady and aimed at the tree. She fired and the bullet hit the trunk. Doc was surprised. She'd been a natural shot, better than a lot of men he knew.

She laughed and said, "That's a good gun, Daddy. But old Hank is sure gonna be mad when he finds out what kind of dog you traded it for."

Doc laughed with her. It wasn't his fault the old man had wanted that dog so bad. It had been a good coon dog, in its earlier years. The dog had died almost a month later after the trade. But he'd tried to tell the old man she was on her last legs.

"Mr. Muroc?"

Doc's head jerked up and he stared at a tall, good looking young man. He stared back down at the gun in his hand. He put it in the nightstand drawer and said, "Yup, that's me."

"Glad to meet you, Mr. Muroc," the young man said, walking towards him with hand extended. "I'm Frank Jones."

"Call me Doc," he said and shook his hand.

"Oh," Frank said. "How are you?"

"Doin' alright," he replied. "You?"

"Fine, fine," he said nervously. "Would you like to go into the living room and talk?"

"We can," he said.

They went into the living room. Frank sat on the couch and Doc took the chair near the window. They didn't say anything for a moment, then Frank sputtered, "Where...I mean...do you know where she might be?"

"No," he said. "That's why I'm here."

Frank nodded. "Uh... Listen, I don't know what's happened, but I want you to know that I won't stop until I find her."

Doc nodded and stared at the young man. He was very clean looking, even his fingernails were buffed and shining. He was broad-shouldered and handsome but Doc knew he'd never done a day's work in his life. But his appearance was deceiving. Frank had worked hard in a steel mill for years and saved everything he had in order to open his insurance agency. He'd only been seeing Ella for about a year.

"I don't know what to say other than that," Frank said. "And, of course, you haven't heard... I mean, you... Have you heard anything from her?"

"No," Doc replied dryly, still unsure of the man. He sat back and studied him. He'd let him do the talking. If he'd done anything he'd give himself up, Doc knew. All he had to do was wait.

Frank got up and began to pace, saying, "I've been sick since she didn't come back. I've made a dozen phone calls, talked to everyone I know and s*he* knows. No one knows anything."

Doc watched him, then his eyebrows rose when Frank stopped pacing abruptly and turned to him. Doc looked into his eyes and immediately felt let down. This boy hadn't hurt Ella. He was too in love with her, too hurt over her disappearance.

"It just frustrates me, Doc," he said. "I sometimes think that someone…" He stopped.

"What?" Doc asked.

He stared at him. "I don't want to say it."

"No, say it, boy."

Frank sat back down on the couch and leaned forward, towards Doc. "Ella was the sweetest, most beautiful woman I've ever known. I can't think of a single person that might want…you know, to hurt her. But in the back of my mind— and I hate to say it—I have a bad feeling that someone did."

Doc nodded. He didn't like Frank saying that, but all Frank had done was to confirm his own suspicions.

"If someone hurt her," Frank said. "I swear to you, I will hunt them down and they will pay dearly. And I won't stop until I find them."

That had been Doc's plan, too.

"I will promise you that, Doc," he told him. "I will promise you that the person who did this will pay."

Doc studied him, then said, just to throw him off, "How do I know it wasn't you?"

Frank didn't seem surprised at his question. "You don't. But I can assure you that it wasn't me, I swear. For all I know, it was you. You see what I'm saying?"

Doc nodded.

"We have to do it together," Frank said. "You and I have to find Ella."

Doc didn't want any help. He could do well on his own. He'd found many things in his life, tracked many animals. His nose, as they say, was better than a bloodhound's. He would find his daughter without the assistance of anyone. It was his duty as her father. He owed it to her.

"I've got a private detective on it," Frank said.

"Don't need one," Doc replied and stood.

"Don't need one?" Frank asked. "Why? He's the best."

"But I don't need him," Doc said and shook his head. He didn't like the thought of some stranger nosing around about his daughter. He didn't like the idea of anyone finding anything out about her. It was his job, as her father, to find her and to protect her as best he could. He knew the detective might have more resources but it was his duty.

Frank was taken aback by Doc's abrupt words and manner. He was flabbergasted to see him go to the door without another word. Frank stood up and asked, "Where are you going?"

"Nothing here," he said. "I'm going back home. I got to work tonight."

"Do you have a car?" Frank asked. "I didn't see one outside."

"Nope, I got a truck," Doc said at the door. "But it wouldn't make it down here, so I took the train."

"Let me drive you," Frank said, rushing after him.

"No, that's alright," Doc said.

"No, I insist."

Doc considered. He'd get home much quicker in a car than that old train. He might have a few hours to rest, even.

"Please," Frank said. "I'd like to talk to you some more."

"Boy, I can take the train back. It's a long drive to Cumberland Gap and the roads are bad."

"I want to go," he said. "I want to meet her mother, too and her brothers and sisters. I was going to come with her that day but I got caught up at work. God, I wished I'd gone with her. I told myself to go, you know? I said to myself, 'This is important, just go.' But I didn't. I was foolish."

Doc nodded. He also felt foolish for the way he'd treated Ella, for the things he'd done and said. He wished he could take every bad word back, every rock he'd thrown at her that day. He wished he could just see her. He'd hug her if he could. He didn't often show affection but promised himself the next time he saw his girl, he'd give her a kiss and a hug, just to show her how much he loved her.

"Please," Frank said. "I'm sick of being alone."

Doc nodded. "If you want to."

Frank smiled. Doc nodded at him once and walked out the door. For a moment, he thought about leaving that Miss Sinclair a note or something saying he was leaving, then said to hell with it and walked outside. But then, he thought about the box of pictures and went back inside and took them out of the closet. Frank didn't say anything when he did that. He eyed the box and smiled slightly to himself. He knew what was in the box and he felt that Doc should have it.

"Let's go," Frank said.

They walked out to the car and Doc's eyebrows rose a little when he saw it. It was the fanciest car he'd ever seen and he'd certainly never ridden in one. It was a nice one, a Cadillac.

"I'm going to get Ella one, too," Frank said and opened the passenger door. "She loves to drive this car."

Doc understood why. But then he hadn't known she could drive at all.

"I taught her to drive," Frank said and motioned Doc into the car. "She got her license and everything."

Doc's eyebrows raised a little but he didn't say a word and got into the car. Frank slammed the door and raced over to the driver's side, got in and put the car in gear. It pulled away from the curb and then Frank punched the gas. The car took off quickly and smoothly. Doc nodded with appreciation and awe.

"Yeah," Frank said, smiling in memory. "Ella loves to drive. You know, the first time I let her, she almost ran into a light pole. But she got better. Actually I think now she drives better than I do."

"That so?" Doc said and thought about it. There were so many things he didn't know about his own daughter.

"Uh huh," Frank said. "In fact, I wanted her to take the car home."

Doc turned to stare at him.

"Shit," Frank muttered. "She wouldn't do it, said she might wreck it or something, like I care."

Doc nodded and stared out the window. He couldn't wait to get home. While he didn't feel uncomfortable with Frank or in his car, he wanted to talk to Ruth, to tell he what he'd found out about those people in New York who had taken Ella's baby.

As if reading his mind, Frank said, "I knew about the baby. She told me about little Olivia. You can talk about it if you like."

"Don't have much to say about that," he muttered, still looking out of the window.

"All I know is what she told me," Frank said. "About Olivia being with the Green's in New York. They take good care of her, from what I understand."

Doc turned to him. "You think them people up there hurt her?"

"No," Frank said. "I mean, I didn't know them and Ella had pretty much stopped going up there by the time we met. But from what she said, they were nice people, good people."

Doc nodded. They sounded like good people, but you could never be sure.

"August twelfth," Frank muttered out of nowhere.

"What?"

"We were getting married on August twelfth," he said. "We had it all planned. She wanted y'all to come down. We were going to get married in this church I used to go to when I was a kid. And afterwards, we were going to have a reception."

"Why didn't she tell us that?"

"She wanted it to be a surprise."

"Oh," Doc muttered, then, "Listen, boy, I have to work tonight and I need some sleep. You don't mind if I shut my eyes for a bit, do you?"

"No, not at all," Frank said and smiled at him.

Doc nodded and closed his eyes. He was exhausted, both mentally and physically, and he dreaded the long night ahead in the mines. He soon fell into a deep sleep and didn't remember any of the ride home.

The Man in the Window

Sleep had taken Doc over and before he knew it, Frank was nudging him awake. He awoke with a start and stared at Frank.

"Sorry, Doc," Frank said. "But I don't know where to go now."

Doc shook his head and rubbed at his groggy eyes and said, "You still on highway twenty-five, ain't ya?"

"Yes."

"Keep going straight," Doc said and sat up.

Frank kept driving and when they reached the road that lead down into the Gap, Doc pointed. "Right here. Turn right here."

Frank made the turn and they drove down the winding road.

"Now turn here," Doc said.

Frank turned and they drove for a little while until they came to the house.

"Now stop," Doc said.

Frank stopped the car in front of the house. He smiled at it, thinking about Ella growing up there, becoming the woman she was. He said, "Nice place."

"It's alright," Doc said and got out. "Come on into the house. Ruth will want to meet you."

Frank got out and followed Doc into the house. Before they got to the front door, the door banged open and the twins ran screaming out, "Daddy's home!" He watched as Doc smiled a little at them and smiled himself when they flung themselves at him, grabbing onto him, almost wrestling him. It was an aggressive display of affection which Doc obviously enjoyed. Two older girls came out calling, "Daddy!" But when they saw Frank, they stopped abruptly and seemed embarrassed. That must be Irene and Susie, he thought.

"This here's Frank Jones," Doc said.

"Who's he?" Roy asked, eying him.

"Reckon he's your sister's fella," Doc said and went into the house, almost colliding with Ruth who was wearing an apron and wiping her hands on a towel.

"You're home," she said, then glanced at Frank. "Why, is this Frank?"

Frank nodded and grinned sheepishly.

"Oh," she said. "Doc, you brought Frank home!"

"He just drove me," Doc said. "Come in, Frank, come on. Boys! Straighten up!"

The twins, who had been scrutinizing Frank since the moment they laid eyes on him, jumped a little at Doc's words. Doc told them to "straighten up" again and went into the kitchen to wash up.

"Oh, their names are Ray and Roy," Ruth said. "And the girls are Irene and Susie. Susie's the littler one."

Frank smiled at the children and said, "Nice to meet you."

They nodded shyly and ducked their heads.

"Now come on in," she said, opening the screen door. "Girls, come in and help me get some coffee!"

Frank smiled at her, then at the children and walked into the house. He looked around. It was clean and comfortable, much like Ella's apartment. It was apparent that the Muroc's didn't have much money but they did have a radio and two couches and a small, pot-bellied stove.

"Girls, go in to the kitchen and put a pot of coffee on," she said.

The girls walked around Frank shyly, then raced into the kitchen. Frank stared after them and said, "They're very pretty girls."

"They're a handful," Ruth said. "But not as bad as the twins."

He nodded.

"Oh, please sit down," Ruth said, smiling deeply at him.

Frank sat on the couch and felt slightly uncomfortable, as any stranger going into an unfamiliar house would.

"Coffee's on, Mommy," Irene said, coming back into the room.

"Daddy already done it," Susie added.

Ruth nodded at them and sat down on the other couch. "I have to say this, and forgive me for doing it, Frank, but you're as handsome as Ella said. Ain't he, Irene? Susie?"

The two girls eyed him as well. They'd never seen such a dapper looking man in their lives. They were both suddenly very jealous of their sister and of the life she had been leading in Knoxville. They felt a little resentment over the fact that they were still stuck in the Gap going to school and helping their mother in the garden and kitchen. They couldn't wait to move on.

"So, tell me a little about yourself Frank," Ruth said and sat back on the couch, then sat back up. "Are you hungry? Let me get you something to eat. I don't know where my manners are."

"I'm fine," Frank said quickly, not wanting her to leave the room. He wanted to ask her some questions, too.

"Sure?" she asked. When he nodded, she smiled again. "Well, let me just say that I was very happy when Ella told me she was getting married."

He nodded. He'd been very happy when she'd accepted.

She leaned in and whispered, "She'd told me about the wedding. I didn't tell Doc cause she wanted to surprise him."

"I told him," Frank said.

"Oh," she said and sat back up, then glanced at the twins, who had come into the room and were standing next to the stove. "Boys, go get Frank a cup of coffee."

"Already got it," Doc said and brought Frank in a steaming cup of coffee. "You take sugar? Milk?"

"Black," Frank said and took the cup. "Thank you."

Doc nodded and sat on the couch beside Ruth.

"So," Frank said. "I think we all know why I'm here."

Ruth nodded. "We do and we appreciate you coming."

"I would have come sooner," Frank said. "But I just... I couldn't. I mean, I could have but I was busy, looking, you know."

Ruth nodded. "Well, you're here now, that's all that matters."

"I don't know what to say," Frank said and put the coffee cup on the table beside the couch. "Doc and I have discussed this in depth and we're both still somewhat unsure of what's happened."

"Uh huh," Ruth said. "What do you think happened?"

"I wish I knew," he said. "I wish I knew."

"Me too," Ruth muttered, looking down.

"Just to let you know," Frank said. "I have hired a private detective and have alerted the police. We're going to find her, Mrs. Muroc."

Ruth smiled at him. She liked his straight-forward attitude and the fact that he called her Mrs. Muroc. No one ever called her that.

"I told you to call that detective off," Doc said.

Frank glanced at him and nodded. "Uh, yeah, we discussed that in the car."

"I don't think you should," Ruth said, glancing sideways at Doc. "I think a private detective might be able to find something out we wouldn't."

"There ain't no need in it," Doc said. "I'm gonna find her myself."

Ruth glared at him. "It won't hurt nothing."

"Maybe," Doc said, thinking it over again, then stared at the twins. "You boys feed the dogs?"

"Not yet," Ray said.

"Get to it," he said, then stared at the girls. "You girls need to get in that kitchen and clean up the supper dishes for your mommy. Go on now."

The girls groaned and left the room. As soon as they were gone, Doc turned to Ruth and said, "I don't want them kids knowing any more than they do right now. There ain't no need in worrying them."

Ruth nodded and glanced at Frank. "He's right. They've been sick with worry about Ella. They talk about her every day, all the time."

Frank said, "We are going to find her, Mrs. Muroc. Mark my word, we are going to find her. I promise."

"I'm glad," Ruth said, sighing with relief that someone had promised to find her child.

Irene came back into the room and said, "Mommy, there's no dish powder."

"I'll get it in a minute," she said. "Are you sure you wouldn't like something to eat, Frank? We've got plenty."

"No, thank you," Frank said. "I actually need to get back before dark."

"You can spend the night," Irene said suddenly.

Doc narrowed his eyes at her and shook his head. She sunk back into the wall.

"Yes, you could do that," Ruth said. "We've got plenty of beds."

"Oh, no thank you," Frank said and stood. "That's very kind of you, though."

Ruth nodded and smiled. "Well, we're always here, Frank. Anytime you want to come here, you come. Don't even think twice about it."

Frank smiled his appreciation at her offer. "I will. Thank you, Mrs. Muroc."

"You're very welcome," Ruth said sweetly and held out her hand. "It was good to meet you, Frank."

Frank shook her hand and said, "You too."

They smiled at each other and Doc got up and walked Frank out to his car. As he opened the door, he said, "Doc, I think the private detective should stay on the case."

"No," Doc said. "I'll find her myself."

Frank began, "I just don't—"

"Listen, boy," Doc said, cutting him off. "I don't trust them people. Plenty of my people in the mines were done in by the likes of private detectives."

Frank stared at him and nodded, remembering hearing stories about the conflict in the mines and how mine companies had used private detectives to control and intimidate the miners. He had heard stories of people being shot to death inside of their homes, about the uprising of the workers who only wanted decent wages so they could feed their families. There had been many people killed during that time. He suddenly understood why Doc felt this way.

"Okay," Frank said. "Just let me know if I can do anything."

"I will," Doc said.

"Oh, wait a minute," Frank said and reached over and picked up the box Doc had brought. "You forgot this."

Doc took it and then waved to him without another word. He took the box to the little shack out back and stashed it there then went back into the house. Ruth was at the window, staring out at the car. As soon as it pulled away, she turned to Doc and said, "That boy didn't hurt her."

Doc knew this already. He'd known it since he first laid eyes on him.

"What happened to her?" she asked. "What the hell happened to her?"

That's what Doc wondered too. He imagined many horrible things. He imagined Ella tied in a basement. He imagined those people in New York beating her. Those people had something to do with it. That was the only explanation. He would like to go to New York and find out for himself. And while he was at it, he'd like to get that baby back, too. But he still had a family to feed and couldn't do much of nothing. He felt limp suddenly, like someone had drained all the energy out of his body. The impending night of hard work might have been what caused it.

He sighed and said, "I got to get ready for work."

"Why don't you take the night off?" she said. "You've been gone all day."

Doc shook his head. He knew he'd have a sleepless night, as he'd had ever since Ella had disappeared. He would rather work. It would take his mind off everything else.

"We'll find her," Ruth said. "Won't we?"

Doc nodded and muttered, "One way or the other," before going back outside.

"Where you going?" Ruth called.

He ignored her and went into the shack and found Ella's suitcases. They hadn't been touched. Inside were her clothes and some gifts for the twins—small cars. He smiled. She still thought they were babies. He emptied the suitcases and rummaged around, not sure of what he was looking for. Then he felt the liner. Sure enough, something was inside of it.

He ripped it apart and found an envelope stuffed with money. There was over a thousand dollars in that envelope. Doc stared at the money, then at the ceiling of the building wondering what the hell was going on. What had Ella been involved in? You just don't have a thousand dollars lying around in a suitcase.

He turned his eye on the box. He opened it and looked through the pictures, feeling that lump rise in his throat again when he saw one of Ella holding the baby up laughing, looking so happy, so young and beautiful. He'd been a fool to make her give that baby up. He should have said to hell with what everyone else thought and told her to stay home and have it.

"What are you doin'?"

It was Ruth. She stood in the doorway, staring at him. He stared back and took the pictures over to her. "I found these here."

She studied the pictures. Tears began to stream down her cheeks. She didn't say anything for a while, then she said, "Pretty baby, ain't it?"

He nodded and took the pictures back.

"Where did you get these?"

"At her apartment."

"You shouldn't have taken those from her apartment," she said.

"I reckon I'm her daddy and I can do whatever I want," he said.

She eyed him and looked back down at the pictures. "Oh, Doc, look at the baby. Look at her!"

Doc nodded and looked away.

"What a beautiful child," she said. "Looks just like a little Indian with all that dark hair, don't she? And she ought to. My mamaw was full-blooded Cherokee. I reckon it carries over, don't it?"

Doc nodded.

"My, oh, my," she muttered, shaking her head.

"I found this, too," he said and handed her the envelope.

Her mouth dropped at all the money. "Where did this come from?"

"I don't know," he said.

Ruth sat down on a bucket and stared up at him. "Doc, where did this come from?"

"I don't know," he said again, then recounted, sparingly, the story the girl at the home had told him.

Ruth listened with wide eyes, gasping from time to time. When he finished the story, she said, "Doc, do you really think she's up there?"

He nodded. He was sure of it.

"Then why didn't that Miss Abernathy tell the police?"

He hadn't thought of that. Why hadn't she? There were gaps in the story, in his reasoning. But he was blind to reason at that point. The only thing he could fathom was that these people in New York had hurt his girl. And for that, they were going to pay.

He got up and took the money out of Ruth's hand and put it in his pocket. She watched him but didn't say a word, then got up to help him put the stuff back into the suitcases and close them up. She reached for the box of pictures at the same time he did, but she got it first.

"What are you doing with that?" he asked, miffed that she was taking it from him.

"It's my girl's box," she said. "I got about as much right to it as anyone else."

He nodded. "I guess you know what I'm going to do now."

"You're going to New York?"

He nodded again. "That alright?"

"Yes," she said. "Just bring her back, Doc, that's all I ask."

"I will," he said. "But I got to go back to Knoxville first."

The next day, he went back to Ella's apartment for the gun. He had to ask Miss Sinclair let him in, which she did after chastising him for leaving "so soon." He only half-listened to her. He was about to fall over from exhaustion from working the previous night and his knees and back were killing him.

"And you left the door unlocked," she tutted. "Oh, did you meet Mr. Jones?"

He nodded.

"Nice young man," she said, smiling. "Ella's very lucky to have him."

Doc didn't answer and went past her into the bedroom, got the gun and stuck it in his jacket. It was a big gun and he didn't like carrying it around like that, but he didn't have much choice.

When he came back out, Miss Sinclair was standing in the living room, looking around.

"I got what I needed," he said.

She smiled at him and nodded, then opened her hand, palm up. "Oh, by the way, I want you to have a key."

Doc took the key out of her hand and slipped it in his pocket.

"That way, if you need to get in, you can," she said. "In case I'm not here."

"Thank you, ma'am," he muttered then pulled the business card out of his wallet and handed it to her. "You know where this fella is?"

She took the card and shook her head. "Dean Bellows, Attorney at Law...ummm... I don't know him, of course, but I do know the address. Do you want me to take you there? I have a car."

"I'd appreciate it."

She smiled, loving that she was having a little adventure, then told him she'd be right back, that she needed to get her handbag and hat. "Can't go out of the house without a hat, Mr. Muroc," she told him and left the apartment.

Doc waited outside until she backed a black Ford out of the driveway. He had an impulse to ask her to let him drive, but dismissed it and got into the car.

Miss Sinclair chatted as they drove through town. Doc ignored her and looked out the window. Soon, they pulled up to a little brick building that had a sign in front: Dean Bellows, Attorney at Law.

"Be right back," Doc said and got out. He walked into the office and looked around. There were a few empty chairs in the reception area and a secretary typing at a desk. He walked up to her and said, "I need to see Dean Bellows."

"And do you have an appointment, Mr....?"

"No," he said. "I just need to see him."

She eyed him and shook her head, then buzzed Mr. Bellows. "There's a man here to see you, sir," she said, then put her hand over the phone. "What was your name?"

"Doc Muroc," he told her.

Her eyebrows raised a little, but she turned her attention back to the phone. "A Mr. Muroc," she said. "Okay. Will do." She hung up and said, "He'll be with you in a few minutes. You can sit over there."

Doc sat in one of the chairs and waited for about ten minutes. Every so often, he'd catch the secretary staring at him, but as soon as he'd look over, she'd turn away abruptly. Doc ignored her and soon Mr. Bellows came out. He stopped at the desk and stared at Doc. He knew what he wanted and wished he hadn't come to him.

"Dean Bellows," he said, walking towards Doc, extending his hand.

"Doc Muroc," Doc said and stood, shaking the man's hand. "I just need a minute of your time, sir."

Dean nodded and they walked into his office where he sat at his desk. "Please sit down."

Doc sat down.

"What can I do for you?"

Doc pulled a picture of Ella out of his pocket and handed it to the man. "That's my girl and I reckon you helped her give her baby away. Her name's Ella Muroc."

Dean eyed him for a moment before picking up the picture. He looked it over and nodded. "I heard, of course, that Ella had disappeared but I haven't talked to her in...in...uh...in a while."

"I know," Doc said. "But them people she gave the baby to is what I'm interested in."

"I can't help you with that," he said and handed the picture back.

"Oh, I think you can," Doc said and slid the picture back into his jacket. "I want to know their name and where they live."

"Absolutely not."

Doc stared at him. "You ain't gonna tell me?"

"I can't," he said. "It was a closed adoption. I'm forbidden by law to talk about it. And it's been so long, I can't remember any of the details."

Doc knew the lawyer was lying, as lawyers tend to do. He knew the man thought of him as some illiterate hillbilly but he didn't care. He had come for information and he wouldn't leave without it.

"Now, if you'll excuse me," Dean said and stood. "I have work to do."

"Sit back down," Doc said and pulled the gun out. "Go on, sit back down."

Dean seemed shaken at the sight of the gun. But he sat back down.

Doc held the gun on the man and said, "I ain't no killer, Mr. Bellows, but I need to know them people's name. I don't care about you and I don't care if I shoot you or not. You're gonna give me that name or you're gonna die."

Dean Bellows was shocked. But he relented and gave up the information, saying, "I am not liable for giving you this information, Mr. Muroc. If it ever comes back to me, I'll tell them how you got it and you'll serve time."

"I reckon I will," he muttered and left the office without another word and got into Miss Sinclair's car.

"Did you get what you needed?" she asked pleasantly.

"I did," he replied. "Can you take me back to the apartment? I need to use the phone."

As soon as he got back to Ella's apartment, he asked Miss Sinclair to show him how the phone worked. She smiled gently at him and showed him.

"That all I need to do?" he asked.

She nodded. "If you have the number, I can make the call for you."

"That's alright," he said. "I think I can handle it myself."

She got the hint but had to say, "It's no trouble."

"I know that," Doc said. "You've been mighty kind to me and I appreciate it."

"I'll leave you to it," she said and backed out of the room. "Let me know if I can do anything."

Doc called Lawson's grocery and told Melvin he needed to speak to Ruth and that he'd call back in thirty minutes. Then he put the gun away and washed up in Ella's bathroom. After that, he went to her refrigerator and pulled the bologna out. He sniffed it, ascertained it was edible, and sat down at the small table and finished it off. Then he got a drink of water at the sink and looked out the window and onto the street.

The street was lined with a sidewalk which was lined with trees, which were in full bloom. It was a nice, pretty street with no garbage or abundance of cars.

Doc was about to turn away when he spotted a man standing in front of the house, staring at it, not moving. Doc studied him for some time. The man was dressed in a beige summer suit and wore a hat. Something told Doc to talk to the man and he was about to wave at him when the man caught him staring and then he walked off quickly. Actually, he limped off. Doc was about to go after him when the phone rang.

"It's me," Ruth said.

"Let me call you back," Doc said. "We can't afford that."

They hung up and he called her back, saying, "I ain't gonna be home tonight. I'm going to New York."

"What did you find out?"

"I found out where them people live," he said. "I'm gonna get a train. I don't know when I'll be back or if I'll be able to call."

"Oh," she said and took a breath. "Alright, you go do what you need to do. You took that money with you, didn't you?"

"Yeah."

"Be careful," she said. "And I'll be praying."

He hung up and then left the apartment quickly, locking the door on his way out. He ran down the street in search of the man in the window but he was nowhere to be found.

New York City

New York City, or even the thought of it, had never impressed Doc. Like most people from Cumberland Gap, he knew it existed but never felt compelled to go and explore it. He had seen pictures of it, but nothing prepared him for the shock of its size. However, it didn't intimidate him in the least and he fell in step with everyone else as they got off the train.

He walked out of Grand Central Station not knowing where he was going. Once out of the station, the city streets confused him and all he had to go on was an address on some street called "Park Avenue." He hurried along, sure he'd come up on the street on his own and as he walked, he would find himself glancing up at the monstrous buildings. *How did they get up there to build them?*

He thought about Ella coming here by herself and having her baby. He felt proud of her for doing that. She was such a smart girl.

Finally, he noticed the taxis on the street, like yellow jackets in a sea of vehicles. People were getting in and out of them. He had the money, so he flagged one down, imitating what he had seen another man do, and got into the backseat.

"Where to, buddy?" the cab driver asked.

Doc took out the address and handed it to the driver. "Here."

The driver looked the address over, then looked Doc over. He'd never seen a man in a pair of work overalls and a nice brand fedora taking a taxi before. Especially not one wanting to go to Park Avenue. He had to ask, "You're not from around here, are you?"

"Just looking for my girl," Doc replied and sat back.

"She on Park Avenue?" the driver asked and pulled away from the curb.

Doc shrugged. He hoped she was on Park Avenue.

The driver kept talking and asking questions, which Doc avoided. He'd only grunt ever so often and soon the driver just gave up. In no time, it seemed to Doc, they pulled up to a big, fancy building with gargoyles on all sides protecting it from evil spirits. It was so tall, it was hard to see the top of it from the street. He pointed at it and said, "There it is."

Doc nodded, looking at the place in awe. Was that where his grandbaby was?

The driver asked for the fare and Doc gave it to him, carefully counting it out. Once he was done, the driver shook his head and chuckled, not caring if he got a tip or not and said, "You have a good day, sir."

"You too," Doc said and got out. Once he reached the door, a man in an odd looking red and black suit came rushing out to him and blocked him from entering.

"How may I help you, sir?"

Doc looked at him and asked, "You know Freddy and Marge Green?"

"Of course," he said. "And do you have business with Mr. and Mrs. Green?"

Doc studied him, wondering what he would have to say to get inside the building and up to their apartment. He couldn't think of a thing and stood there mute.

"Do you have business with the Greens'?" the doorman asked again, staring at him and at his clothes. He was real clean but dressed oddly for New York. Was this man a vagrant? A conman? Perhaps he was a common workman there to do some plumbing or something.

"I do," he said. "But I can't tell you about it."

The doorman knew he would definitely not let him in.

Doc leaned in and whispered, "I can give you some money if you tell me where to find them. Now, I don't mean no harm, so you won't have to worry about that. I just need to talk to them, that's all."

"Where are you from, sir?" he asked and stared at him. The man looked almost frazzled, almost in a panic about something. He suddenly felt compelled to help him but he didn't know why. Some people you automatically want to help and others you wouldn't give the time of day. Funny how that worked.

"Cumberland Gap, Tennessee," he told him.

The doorman nodded, taking it all into consideration. He was sure this man meant no harm, whoever he was, so he leaned in and whispered, "Mr. Green is out of town on business."

Doc felt his shoulders slump.

"But Mrs. Green takes her daughter to the park on Wednesday and Thursday afternoons to give the nannies a break."

It was now Wednesday afternoon. Doc asked the man, "So they there now?"

He nodded.

Doc looked around. "What park?"

"Central Park, sir," he said.

"Thank you," Doc said and reached into his pocket and pulled out a five-dollar bill, which he handed the man.

The doorman took the bill and started to put it in his pocket, but felt a surge of guilt. He wasn't that desperate for money, even if he was a working man. He handed the money back and said, "It's been a pleasure, sir."

Doc stared at the money and then at the man, confused. But then he shrugged and started off in the wrong direction. The doorman watched him go, then shook his head, walked after Doc and called, "It's not that way, sir."

Doc cursed under his breath and turned back to the man. He was getting frustrated at all the traffic, people and confusion. He just wanted to find his daughter, that's all.

The doorman pointed across the street to the park. Doc stared in that direction, then said, "And she's in there?"

The doorman nodded.

Now this looked daunting. Sure, there were streams of people coming in and out of the park but suddenly Doc was in a panic. How would he ever find a woman he'd never seen before in a park that size? It was bigger than all of Cumberland Gap, probably, and a lot more intimidating.

"Mrs. Green is wearing a yellow dress today," the doorman said. "Just keep walking straight until you come to the pond. That's where she is."

Doc nodded and thanked the man, then he took a breath and crossed the street and started walking. He walked and walked until he came upon the pond. It was a huge pond and pretty. There were people all around it, laughing and enjoying the sunny day. Doc felt tired and sat down on a bench and looked around. He felt anxious that he wouldn't find Mrs. Green.

"Say a prayer for me, Ruth," he muttered, still looking around. "Say a prayer for me."

Fifteen minutes passed and nothing happened. There were too many people around. Doc studied every last one of them but didn't see a yellow dress or a little girl. He felt a surge of panic again, but dismissed it. They were here; they had to be here somewhere. There were too many people around, though. Too many possibilities.

"Say a prayer for me," he muttered again but felt foolish. But then, as if his prayer had been answered, a little girl walked by with an ice cream cone. She stopped right in front of Doc and stared him dead in the eye.

Doc nearly came up off the bench. Her blue eyes looked just like her mother's. He knew it was Ella's child but it was as if he'd seen a ghost. A memory of her stopping in front of his chair at that age and putting her hand on her hip came back to him. She had said, "Daddy, Mommy wants you in the kitchen now. She needs you to cut the turkey." It had been Thanksgiving and he'd killed a wild turkey for them to eat. Ruth had worked on it all morning, basting it, trying to get the "wild taste" out and had pretty much succeeded.

The little girl licked her ice cream and continued to stare at him. Doc stared back and had an urge to grab her and to run all the way back to Cumberland Gap. He could do it. He could take her back to Ruth. Ruth could raise her as her own. But he didn't. Nor did he have time. Out of nowhere a woman in a yellow dress came rushing up to them. "Olivia!"

The child jerked and stared around at her furious mother, and then, as if she'd forgotten about her existence, muttered, "Oh, no."

It was all Doc could do to keep from laughing.

"Olivia!" she screeched and ran up and grabbed her arm. "I told you not to run away from me!"

Olivia didn't answer and stared back at Doc.

"Is she bothering you, sir?" Mrs. Green asked.

He shook his head.

"Pardon," she said and bent down to Olivia. "Let me tell you one thing, little girl, if you run off again, we're not coming back to the park!"

Olivia nodded and said, "I'm sorry, Mommy, but it's funny to see you run."

Mrs. Green almost smiled, but caught herself just in time. She started to reprimand her more, but another little girl came running up, yelling, "Olivia!"

"Oh, God," Mrs. Green muttered. "I forgot about her. How could I have forgotten about her?"

Olivia jumped, dropping her ice cream and ran to the little girl. They grabbed each other and hugged, then ran off together.

Mrs. Green sat down in exhaustion and said, "I should know better than to bring two little girls to the park at once."

Doc nodded. "They both your kids?"

She turned and looked at him, then smiled deeply, eying his fedora and overalls. "Oh, you're from the south, aren't you? How lovely. What brings you to New York?"

Doc shrugged and said, "Is both them kids yours?"

"Oh, no," she said and waved her hand. "Olivia, the one with the ice cream, is mine and the other little girl is our neighbor. They've been friends since they were newborns."

Doc blanched. That stung. He didn't like to know about Olivia's friends. He didn't like the thought of someone else getting her smiles or hugs. He wanted her all to himself. She was his blood and she belonged to him.

"Pretty girl," he muttered, still staring at Olivia. She looked just like Ella at that age.

She stared after Olivia and smiled pleasantly. "She's a lovely child. Sometimes she's a handful but all in all, she's a pure delight."

For a second, Doc wanted to ask her how much she paid for Olivia. He knew how those girls' homes worked and he knew that people paid money for those babies. He was not cold-hearted but when it came to his family, he could be. He'd do anything to protect them. But then a thought crossed his mind. He hadn't protected Ella, had he? No. He had sent her out into the cold to atone for her sins. A strong, overwhelming urge to protect Olivia overcame him. The urge to kidnap her was just as strong. He wouldn't do it, of course, that's not the way things worked, but he wanted to. Maybe, in part, just to make it up to Ella.

Mrs. Green turned to him and said, "So, what brings you to New York?"

Doc stared at her and something told him that she hadn't done anything to Ella either. It was a letdown but a letdown he was happy to feel. He knew, also, that Olivia was in good hands. This woman's manner told him as much. She was kind and caring and pretty, with long limbs and blond hair. And he didn't want to bring her into all this. Most of all, he didn't want Olivia to know something might have happened to her mother. In ignorance, there is bliss and Doc wanted Olivia to have all the bliss he was sure she was deserving of, even if it came at the expense of his pride.

Just then, Olivia put a foot into the water, then shivered, hugging herself.

"Olivia!" Mrs. Green yelled. "Get out of the water!"

Olivia got out of the water. For an instant, Doc wanted to tell Mrs. Green that it was no use, that the child would do what she wanted, in part just to spite the parent. That's the way Ella had been. As she got older, she loved her parents and respected them, but as a child, she loved to see how far she could push them, mainly in part because she got such a big kick out of it.

Mrs. Green got up and started to excuse herself, then she turned to Doc. For some reason, she thought he might be homeless and for that she felt bad and had an aching desire to help this old man. From the look of his clothes, he could use some help. "Is there anything you need, sir?"

"No, thank you, ma'am," he said. "I just like to watch the babies play."

She nodded. "How about a cup of soup?"

Doc stared up at her, realizing she was getting too close. He didn't want to tell her what he was doing there or why he'd come, mainly because of how it might affect Olivia. He stood up hurriedly and said, "No, thank you, ma'am. Bye now."

Mrs. Green stared after him for a moment, then heard Olivia squeal. She turned around to see the child holding a frog that a little boy had given her. She yelled, "Goodness gracious, Olivia! That's a new dress!" before hurrying over to her.

Doc walked out of the park and got back on the street. It was odd to him how noisy the city became as soon as he walked out of the park. It had been calm and peaceful there but now it was chaos again.

He didn't know what he would do but he knew he'd probably go on home. He felt defeated, demoralized. He knew the Green's hadn't hurt Ella and he'd probably known that before he came. But none of it made sense, it just didn't add up. *Where could she be?*

As he walked, he noticed that the street had turned into a shopping district of some kind. When he came to a toy store, he stopped in front of it and went in without thought. In a matter of minutes, he had bought the child some toys, a big stuffed bear and some dolls. He felt foolish buying these things, but he wanted to. He felt even more foolish for taking them back to the park and then he felt a letdown of a different kind. They were gone.

That night, Doc got a hotel room but slept fretfully. He awoke early and got up, showered, shaved and dressed, then went down to the little diner he'd eaten supper at yesterday. After breakfast, he went back to the room, gathered the toys and paid his bill.

He hurried on to the park and prayed that they would come back that day. He waited on the same bench. He waited all morning and then, in the afternoon, they finally emerged. Mrs. Green was wearing a blue dress today and she looked lovely.

As soon as he saw them, he rushed up to them and said, "I got these for your kid," and thrust the gifts at Mrs. Green.

"Why...I..." she started but then stopped, narrowing her eyes. "Who are you?"

"I have to go now," he said. "But that's for Olivia."

Olivia was eying the big bag of toys and reached out for them. Mrs. Green held them out of her reach and said, "Olivia, go play."

"But, Mommy—"

"Now," she said.

Olivia sighed and walked off.

Mrs. Green turned on Doc. "Now you hold on. Who are you and what do you want?"

He stared at her, then at Olivia and said, "I'm her granddaddy, that's all. My girl gave you that baby."

She gasped. "You're Ella's father?"

He nodded and started off.

"Wait!" she said and grabbed his arm. "What are you doing here? Why didn't you call first?"

"I don't know," he said and started off again.

"Mr. Muroc," she said, grabbing his arm. "I'm confused. Is there something wrong with Ella?"

"She's gone missing," he said, feeling that old lump rise in his throat again. "I guess I thought you might know something about it."

"Ella's missing?" she asked. "Oh, no. What happened?"

"Don't know," Doc said. "That's why I came up here."

She stared at him, mouth agape and said, "Oh, God...oh, God!"

Doc felt the same way.

"I just don't know what to say," she said. "We haven't seen her in a while, you know? She would come up fairly often but a couple of years ago, she told me that she couldn't do it anymore. She was afraid she'd try to kidnap Olivia or something, which is absurd but still..."

Doc nodded that he understood.

She smiled at him. "Oh, Mr. Muroc, why didn't you tell me yesterday who you were?"

"Didn't seem like I should," he mumbled.

"Ella always spoke so fondly of you," she said. "Young girls always idolize their fathers so."

He didn't feel like she should idolize him, though, not after what he'd put her through. But looking at Olivia and at her apparent happiness, he didn't feel as bad. He knew he couldn't have given Olivia this life and he sure as hell knew Harry Thompson couldn't either. He was glad, so very glad, that Olivia had landed in this family, with this nice woman, even though he still felt an overwhelming desire to take her back home with him.

"If there's anything I can do, let me know," Mrs. Green said.

"There's nothing nobody can do but me," Doc said. "I need to get back home."

"Wait," she said. "Would you like to hold Olivia?"

His head jerked up and he stared at her, feeling undeserving of her kindness. But he did want to hold her. He'd wanted to hold her since the moment he'd laid eyes on her. He nodded slowly.

"Let me get her," she said with a smile. "You go sit down and I'll bring her to you."

Doc went to the bench and sat down. In a matter of minutes, Mrs. Green brought Olivia back, telling her, "This is Ella's daddy. Do you remember Ella?"

Doc almost choked on the tears that came up on him suddenly. But he stopped them just in time.

Olivia stared at her, then at Doc, not answering. She was confused.

"Anyway, he likes you very much and wants to give you a hug. Will you hug him?"

She nodded.

Mrs. Green picked her up and sat her in Doc's lap. He stared into her eyes for a moment before pulling her into a deep hug. She stiffened, then relaxed and said, "You smell funny."

Doc laughed and then kissed her cheek. "I think that's the nicest thing anyone's ever said to me, little girl."

She stared at him in confusion before erupting into playful, little girl giggles that were a delight to Doc's ears.

"She likes you," Mrs. Green said. "She even asked about you last night, wanting to know who that man was in the park."

Doc nodded and stared back at Olivia. She was the prettiest little thing he'd ever seen in his life. He thought about how he'd forced Ella to give this baby up. He thought about how everyone's lives would be if he'd allowed Ella to marry Harry Thompson. She'd be home now. He tried not to think too much about it. It hurt too much to know that he'd driven her away. Yet, looking into Olivia's happy eyes, he was assured, once again, that he had made the right decision. It was pride that made him doubt his decision. But it did hurt an awful lot once the moment was over and he had to give Olivia back to Mrs. Green.

Moving On

Doc went home and went back to work. He found himself going to the river more often where he would sit alone, wondering what he was going to do. He didn't want to bother Ruth with all this. Time was moving on but he didn't give up the search. Frank Jones wrote letters every week, begging him to let him put the private detective back on the case. But Doc knew once he did that, he'd be giving up. And it was his duty to find Ella, not some private detective's. He thought he'd made himself clear and that Frank understood his position, but apparently he hadn't. But Doc knew why Frank kept harping on the private detective. He was worried that too much time was slipping by and with time came even more uncertainly, even more distance put between them and Ella. Whenever Doc thought of it, his stomach would go into knots and he had a hard time breathing.

A year soon passed. During that year, his family was healing even if he wasn't. One day, he walked in on Ruth, who was playing a board game with the twins on the floor of the living room. They were laughing and moving the little pieces around. They were acting like they didn't care anymore. This infuriated him to no end and he kicked the game with his foot. The board and its little pieces went flying.

Ruth and the twins jumped up, startled. "What the hell is wrong with you?"

"What are *you* doing?" he hissed. "Playing a game? Your girl's out there and she needs us and you don't care!"

"Boys," she said calmly. "Go outside."

They stared at their father, then at their mother and nodded. As soon as they left the room, Ruth turned on Doc.

"What's wrong with you?" she asked him.

"What's wrong with you?" he snapped. "You're sitting here acting like nothing's happened!"

"I'm what?" she screeched. "How dare you say that to me? I cry myself to sleep every night!"

He sat down in the chair in a huff. "Just tell me what you're doing, Ruth."

"Moving on," she said. "I guess that's what we're all trying to do, Doc."

He jumped up, ready to slap her for her treason. "How dare you? You don't love her!"

It was not her nature to back down from him, so she stood tall and said, "Don't you dare say that to me. Don't you dare! I love that girl more than anything. And it wasn't me that threw rocks at her, that was you! It wasn't me that ran her out of this house! That was you!"

As she said the last sentence, she pushed a finger against his chest to illustrate her point. Before Doc knew what he was doing, he pushed her. She fell back onto the couch but was up in a second, ready to fight him. They were both so shattered by what had happened, it was miracle this confrontation hadn't come sooner.

"At least you got to see the grandbaby," she said, her voice rising. "I didn't even get that! What did I get? Nothing, as usual! I didn't get anything but laundry and cooking! I didn't get anything but having to send my girl away from home!"

He looked away from her.

"You go to hell, Doc Muroc," she hissed, on the verge of tears. "You go to hell and leave me alone. There ain't nothing I can do and I know it. All I can do is sit back and wonder why God's done this to me. All I can do is cry. All I can do is pray. That's all any of us can do."

She started out of the room but he grabbed her arm and pulled her to him, into a hug. In a matter of seconds, she was sobbing. He let her cry. He was sorry he'd exploded like that, sorry that they were both in this situation. But they were in it together, for better or worse.

As she cried, Doc realized the real reason for his anger was that he was out of money. The money he'd found in Ella's suitcase was all but gone. He'd used every cent of it in his search and then he'd turned to the small savings account he had and used it too. He used every cent he could get his hands on to continue his search. He'd gone as far as Miami, Florida and he only went there because Ella had once told her mother that she'd like to visit. Even as he made the long trip, he knew it was a waste of time. He'd be gone for days, sometimes weeks at a time and was becoming tired of chasing a ghost, though he never let himself believe for one minute that she wasn't alive. That thought would be pushed from his mind whenever it crossed it. But he did have a sneaking suspicion that no matter how far he traveled or how hard he looked, he would not find her. Perhaps it was just self-doubt or maybe it was because he realized the world was a big place and that meant it was big enough for a small girl like Ella to get lost in.

But without money, the search couldn't go on. And he never wanted it to end, not until he found her.

Besides that, the FBI was in on it now, too. They would call and tell him to come somewhere and identify a body. He'd made several of those types of trips, all made in anxious anticipation, sometimes feeling so sick he would almost throw up. He'd get to the morgue of whatever city and the young girl on the table would never be Ella. He thought about those young girls he had seen and wondered where their families were and how they must worry over their daughters. He was glad it was never Ella on those tables but at the same time, it made him worry that this was the way he might someday find her. And, like all fathers, he just didn't want to find his girl that way. He wanted her to be safe and happy and most of all, alive. That's all he wanted, and since he began to want this, he wanted for nothing else but.

"We're out of money," he said. "I can't search no more."

Ruth looked up at him. "What? It's all gone? Even the savings?"

He nodded.

She stepped back from him and said, "Then I know what I have to do."

"What's that?"

"I gotta get the still out, that's what."

Doc stared at her. "I don't want you to do that. You could get caught."

"Better than not knowing," she said. "Anything's better than not knowing what's happened to my girl."

Doc nodded and the next day Ruth took a trip into the woods behind their house. Ruth Muroc was a church-going woman and had always been. She believed in the Lord wholeheartedly. She believed in right and wrong and she didn't believe in drinking for pleasure. The only time she'd ever drank a drop was to fix herself a hot-toddy for colds. She'd even given them to her children.

Money had always been scarce but when it got to the point that her kids were going to go hungry or go without, Ruth did something her father had taught her years and years ago. Without this, many times, there wouldn't have been food on the table or gifts for Christmas. She'd even bought Ella a nice dress to wear and two suitcases when she went away to the girls' home.

But she did it sparingly because she knew it was wrong, though she didn't object to others doing it, as she felt everyone had freewill. And, in cases of emergency, she used her freewill to do what she had to. She would go without for months before she gave into it. It was time to do it again.

Ruth walked for about half a mile into the woods until she came to what looked like a pile of tree branches. She bent over and began to move them, uncovering the still. She steeled herself for the coming task, already missing her kitchen and stove, as the process of making the moonshine took a while. She'd have to spend most of her time there, watching over it. The boys would bring her food and water and they'd help her with it but it would be a while before she would be back in her kitchen.

She got busy. You don't just make moonshine, you create it. And it was a long process. She settled in and prepared her batch. When it was ready to be bootlegged, she got a visit from the sheriff, Billy Norris.

"Well, well, what have we here?" he asked with a smile.

She smiled back. Billy had been in business, on and off, with her kinfolk for years. The first time she made it, she had sent word via her brother to him to see if he was interested in doing business with her, too. Billy had been surprised when he got word that Ruth was making moonshine. She had a reputation of being a good, church-going woman, very devout. He knew her family made it, but Ruth? However you could never tell about people, never know why they did the things they did. Billy understood that Ruth did it to help feed her kids and run her household. That was fine by him.

"Why you doing this, Ruth?" he had asked her years ago when she made her first batch. "You know, it can lead to an awful lot of trouble."

"Doc's been down with his knees two weeks," she said. "You know he fell and busted them up good, don't you?"

He nodded.

"So, we ain't got no paycheck coming in," she said. "The kids are hungry."

He nodded. He'd known the people around there had been making moonshine since they came over from Ireland. He also understood that Ruth wouldn't have been doing it unless it was sheer necessity. The law in Cumberland Gap at that time was "according." The sheriff always took everything into account and turned it over, bending the law when necessary. And right now, the law had to be bent. There were kids that were hungry.

He said, "I have to let you know that you can go to jail for this."

"I reckon I understand," she said.

He nodded. "Fifty-fifty split?"

"Fifty-fifty," she had said and shook his hand, then said mischievously, "And I'll even see you in church on Sunday."

He laughed and she sold her first batch. When Ruth had this moonshine ready this time, she got another visit from Billy Norris.

"Fifty-fifty?" he asked.

"Fifty-fifty," she said.

"You know, Ruth," he said, picking up a Mason jar and holding it to the light. "You make this the best. Why don't you make more and let's get rich?"

"The Lord will provide," she said, smiling at him. "How soon can you get me my money?"

"Give me three days, Ruth," he said. "You make any extra for me?"

"Always do, don't I?" she said and smiled.

In three days, Doc had his money and he started his search again. But now he didn't know where to go. Every place in America seemed like a possibility to him and America was a big place. He waited to set out again, turning possibilities over and over in his mind.

Something told Doc not to go on another wild goose chase. Something told him to head right back to where he started. As he took the train to Knoxville, he didn't realize that his search would end up coming full circle. His search would up leading him right back to where he started, at Miss Sinclair's. And that's where he would find all of his answers.

Everything that Ella was calling out to him to know, he would in time.

And Ella had been calling out to him since the day of her disappearance. He heard her at night and he heard her in the mines. She was in his head, in his heart. She wouldn't let go until he found her. She told him not to give up looking.

He went back to her apartment, which had since been rented out. Miss Sinclair had sent a letter apologizing that she couldn't hold it any longer. She would store Ella's things, though, and when they wanted them, she'd have them ready.

Doc stood in front of the house, looking at the window, remembering the man on the street just last year. The man had never left his mind, either. Just then, a pretty young woman walked by, muttering, "Pardon."

He stepped back and said, "Sorry."

She stopped and turned to him. "You're not... I know this sounds crazy, but you're not Ella Muroc's father, are you?"

"I am."

"Miss Sinclair told me you came by last year," she said. "I wish I could have gotten to meet you then."

He nodded.

"I live here. I mean, I used to. I got married," she said and waved at the house, then introduced herself as Jean Davis, formerly Jean Stephens. "I got married and moved out a few months ago. Ella and I are good friends."

"Nice to meet you," he said.

"No, it's so nice to meet you," she said and came towards him, hand extended.

He shook her hand, thinking about all the new people he'd met in the last year. More people than he'd wanted to meet, that's for sure.

"You know," she said. "Ella showed me a picture of you once, in overalls. You look exactly the same way now. Are those the same overalls?"

"No, these are a different pair."

"What about the hat?"

"It's a different one," he said and touched the tip. It was the hat he'd worn to the train station that day Ella didn't come home. He'd worn it every day since.

She nodded, smiling, then turned to the house. Her smile disappeared. "I come by here ever so often, I don't know why. I come by and think she's gonna show up. Sometimes I stop in to see Miss Sinclair, but mostly, I just walk by and look. Then I leave."

Doc wondered what she was getting at.

"I don't know what I hope to find," she said. "Maybe I'm crazy."

"How long did you know Ella?" he asked.

"For a few years," she said. "She and I started working at Patterson Enterprises together. We were in the secretarial pool."

Doc nodded.

"And then she wanted an apartment and I had lived here for a while," she said. "And there just happened to be one that opened up, so she moved in. We had a lot of fun. We'd talk all night and eat popcorn. We'd go to the movies, too. Ella's a lot of fun."

Doc appreciated her kind words about his daughter and the fact that she didn't use Ella in the past tense.

"But then..." She paused, thinking. "Can I buy you a cup of coffee, sir? I'd like to talk to you about something."

Doc nodded. He wanted to know everything she knew and wondered why no one had told him about this girl in all the time he'd been looking for Ella.

They went to a little diner down the street, settled in and Jean smiled at him. "Are you hungry? I'm hungry. I think I'll get a burger."

"You and Ella come here a lot?" he asked.

"We did," she said. "Especially after a late night. We went dancing a lot."

He stared at her, wondering about that. What kind of dances had they gone to? He thought that Ella shouldn't be out too late, that people might start to talk, but then realized it didn't matter anymore. And for the first time, he wondered why he'd ever concerned himself with worrying about what other people thought of him and his family as it never led to anything but trouble. He knew it was because people got ruined over things that others said about them and that he just wanted to protect his family from wagging tongues. Now he realized their opinions didn't matter, never had. All that mattered was what this girl was going to tell him.

The waitress came by and Jean ordered them both a burger plate and coffee. When she disappeared, she turned to Doc and said, "I'm going to stop beating around the bush now, okay?"

"Okay," he said.

She scratched her face and said, "I know something happened to her. I don't know what, but something did. I don't want to alarm you but I haven't been able to talk, you know?"

"Why not?"

She shrugged lightly and pulled a pack of cigarettes out of her purse. "Would you like one?"

"No, thank you," he said.

She lit the cigarette, inhaled, exhaled and said, "Between you and me, I might know something."

Doc sat up. This was the only person who "knew something." He was eager for the information.

She looked around before she went on in a whisper, "There was this man who liked her a little *too* much, if you know what I mean."

Doc knew.

"But I can't tell anyone," she said. "Or I'd be in trouble. You see, his daddy is very rich and powerful. I was warned to keep my mouth shut."

Doc grew alarmed. Then he thought about the money in the suitcase. Was that where it came from?

"So I have," she said. "And I can't live with myself. I started to come up to your house several times but I couldn't. I don't know, maybe I'm just a coward, Mr. Muroc."

"You're no coward," he said. "Who was this boy?"

She leaned in and whispered, "His name is Charlie Patterson."

That's all Doc needed to know.

Charlie Patterson wasn't hard to find. His family was the richest in Knoxville. He drove a Lincoln and lived in a nice home by himself. He wasn't married and had no children. He didn't seem like a bad man. And in reality, he wasn't that bad. He'd just done a bad thing. No, a few bad things.

But once Doc laid eyes on him, he knew this was the man he needed to talk to. How he knew wasn't apparent other than the fact that it was the same man he had seen in front of Ella's apartment that day, staring in. The man in the window, as he'd started to call him in his mind. The well-dressed man who walked with a limp. He hadn't found Ella's ghost, he'd found Charlie's. But she had led him to Charlie. And within Charlie were all the answers Doc was looking for. In a matter of time, Doc would know exactly what happened and it would be Charlie Patterson himself that would tell him.

Two Years Earlier

The year was probably 1954 or so and Ella was moving up in the world. She'd gotten a good job, a nice apartment and was having fun with her upstairs neighbor, Jean Stephens. Ella thought she'd finally broken through and was about to start living a life that wasn't full of hardship and misery. She was going to make it, she was sure of it.

For all intents and purposes, Ella was not the carefree, happy girl everyone thought she was. Things had happened to her that she'd never tell anyone. She looked happy, though, and everyone assumed she was. She could have been a lot happier if she hadn't made so many foolish choices.

When she'd first come to Knoxville, she'd been withdrawn, backward. She didn't even know how to use the right fork at the dinner table but, because Miss Abernathy insisted all the girls learn table manners, it was only a matter of time before she began to reach for the appropriate one. She'd always shared a bed with her sisters and the first few weeks of having one all to herself took some getting used to. Soon, she began to take a single bed and a salad fork for granted, like some people did. She grew more comfortable with her surroundings and it wasn't long before the old Ella came out and the old Ella liked to have fun.

The girls at the home were filled with guilt and despondency. They cried constantly. Ella, herself, had never been a crier. She had been raised to hold it in. And the other girls began to get on her nerves. Someone was always breaking down. Sure, they had reason enough to do this, but then again, life needed living. They were all going through a rough patch but Ella didn't see any reason why they had to live in a perpetual hell in addition to giving up their babies. Wasn't that, in and of itself, enough? One day, she had had enough and stood up in the living room during group time and said, "We need to have some fun."

Everyone in the room, including Miss Abernathy, stared at her.

"There's this game I heard of," she said. "Croquet. Have you heard of it, Miss Abernathy? I read about it in a book."

She had, in fact, heard of the game. She nodded at Ella.

Ella smiled and said, "Could we get one?"

"I think we might be able to," Miss Abernathy said and smiled at Ella. She liked this young woman, liked her suggestion and the next week, the croquet game was set up in the backyard and all girls played, studying the rule book it came with. They used the mallets to hit the big, festively colored balls and laughed. Miss Abernathy stood back and watched. The girls seemed more alive now. Ella had done a good thing. That was only one of the things Ella did to bring joy into the girls' home.

Miss Abernathy took a keen liking to Ella. The girl had a strong spirit and that's just what the home needed. So, after her baby was born, she asked her to stay on. She'd give her a small salary and she'd send her to secretarial school. Ella, who had wanted to go back home, considered this for a few weeks. After she had thought about it, she knew it was the right thing to do and agreed to stay.

Within a couple of years, she had finished secretarial school and had gotten a job at Patterson Enterprises. She met Jean there and Jean helped her get an apartment. Ella was going to have her own room for the first time in her life. Things were looking up for her and she finally believed in a better future. All that bad stuff was behind her but that didn't keep her from thinking about it and feeling bad about how things had turned out.

When Ella had found out she was pregnant with Harry Thompson's baby, she knew her father would be very upset with her. But was almost nineteen and knew she couldn't stay a child forever. Of course, she felt bad about it but she intended to do the right thing—marry Harry and have the baby.

Except that her father hadn't wanted her to. His reaction to the news of her pregnancy still astonished her. He wanted to send her off! That news was worst than his reaction to finding her and Harry in the woods and that was bad enough. This man, this quiet, somber man had had such a violent reaction, she somehow felt that *she* was bad—real bad—and she deserved what had happened. When he had stoned her, she knew he'd done it out of frustration and because his expectations was that she remain pure until she married. For that, she forgave him. But when he wanted to send her away, she held back from forgiveness. A girl who got pregnant out of wedlock in the late 1940s was a bad girl, that much was true, but did she deserve to be shunned by her own family?

Ella didn't know. All she knew was that she had disappointed her father and that's what she couldn't stand. She tried to dissuade him from sending her off and tried to talk some sense into him about it but to no avail. She'd spent her time trying to make it up to him, trying to convince him that marrying Harry would be the right thing, but he'd just shake his head and leave the room without a word. He'd go days without talking or even looking at her and because of that, she felt lost. But mostly she felt shame.

She finally forced him to talk to her. He was fishing at the river. She came up beside him and sat down on a big rock. They didn't speak for a long time. She decided she'd break the silence since he wasn't going to, so she said, "Daddy, I'm sorry."

Of course, Doc didn't respond. He was sorry, too. Sorry that this had happened to his girl, to his family. He knew everyone was talking about Ella like she was white trash and that he couldn't stand. But what really got him was that he realized she was grown up and there wasn't much he could do about it. He didn't want his daughter in this predicament. He just wanted her safe and free from sharp tongues. He knew she would never live this down, not in a town the size of Cumberland Gap, and the thought of the things people were saying about his child drove him crazy. She ought to have had better sense than to go get mixed up with that sorry Harry Thompson.

Ella sighed and tried again, "Daddy, I mean it, I'm sorry."

"I heard you the first time," he said and reeled in a small fish, which he threw back, then cast the line again.

She looked up at him and felt like crying. "I'm going to do the right thing, you know?"

"What's the right thing, girl?" he asked.

"I'm gonna marry him."

"You are?" he asked. "You love that boy?"

Fact was, she didn't love Harry Thompson. He'd just gotten the best of her one night at a barn dance. She grew embarrassed thinking about how she'd drank a little too much and let him get a little too close. He'd also gotten her that day in the woods. She shuddered with the memory of being caught. It was such an embarrassment and, every time she thought about it, it turned her insides out. She always forced the memory out of her mind.

"Huh?" Doc asked.

"Yeah, I think so," Ella lied. "Besides, what's love anyway?"

"Everything," he said and glanced sideways at her.

Ella sighed loudly, rolled her eyes and said, "Daddy, you're just making this so hard on me. Why are you doing this?"

"I don't know," he muttered, feeling sad. And he didn't know. All he knew was the frustration he felt from the time he woke to the time he went back to sleep. It drove him crazy but there wasn't much he could do about it.

"Well," Ella said, standing. "I tried to talk to you. But I can't. You won't talk to nobody! You just hurt people, Daddy!"

She started off but Doc stopped her and said, "You don't think I want more for you than that?"

"No, I don't," she said.

"Huh," he replied. "So you don't think I want you do something with your life more than Harry Thompson's and babies?"

"What do you mean?" she asked, staring up at him.

"Girl, take a look around here," he said. "What do you see? A river? A mountain? I'll tell you what I see. I see cold winters hauling in firewood and I see mines where I have to crawl on my belly to get to my work every night. I see years put on your mommy's face. That's what I see."

"That doesn't make any sense, Daddy."

"Not now it don't," he said. "You give it a few years and you'll know right quick what I'm talking about."

She glared at him. "You're just an old man, that's all you are and you don't want me to be happy."

"Old man, huh?" he asked and laughed. "You don't know how old I am, do you?"

"Of course I do, Daddy," she said. "You're thirty-nine."

"And you think that's old, don't you?"

"It *is* old," she said.

Her naïveté made him chuckle but then the sour look came back on his face and he shook his head. "I'm thirty-nine years old, Ella, and I know I look a hundred. You can thank the coal mines for that."

She rolled her eyes. "Maybe you just look old for your age."

He laughed again. "Right. How old do you think your mommy is? I'll tell you. She's thirty-five and look at the age on her face. That's from hard work, Ella. We ain't that old, we just look it."

"So?"

"So," he said. "Think about Harry Thompson and them babies you'll have with him. Think about all the work you're gonna do in the next few years. And the work don't ever stop, girl, it don't ever stop. Look at your mommy. She was beautiful when I found her, looked just like you look. Now go home and take a hard look at her face 'cause that's what you're gonna look like in ten years."

Ella swallowed hard. She'd always thought her parents were just old, she hadn't realized they'd aged prematurely from all the hard work. But she had to do what she had to do, so she said, "I don't care, Daddy. I'm gonna get married and I'm gonna have Harry's baby. That's the way it is, the way it has to be. I don't care anymore. I just have to do it."

"I care," he said. "I didn't always look like this. I had girls from three counties chasing after me."

"So?"

"So," he said. "When you and Harry tie the knot, I'm gonna get him a job in the mines."

Ella felt nervous. She'd just wanted reassurance but then, he'd made his point, loud and clear. If she stayed there, she'd end up just like her parents. That was assured. She didn't want that life, but then again, it was all she'd ever known. She had no idea what was out there but she knew she wanted to know. That made her listen to her father and to consider what he had to say.

"I don't want this life for you, Ella," he said. "I want you and the other kids to have a better life than this. I don't know much, but I know there is a good life out there for each of you but if you don't start with it, none of the others will. They'll follow in your footsteps, Susie and Irene and then the twins. You have to get out and set the example."

Ella felt a big responsibility set on her shoulders that day. But she knew her father was right. And there were options. What life could she give a baby? What life could she and Harry make? She didn't love Harry, she didn't even know if she liked him that much or not.

"What can I do?" she asked quietly.

"You have that baby and you give it up," he said. "And then you move as far from here as you can get, girl."

Ella panicked at the idea of leaving her family.

"Maybe one day, you can send for your sisters," he said. "And you can help them, too. But you got to get out. I won't have you waste your life like me and your mommy did."

Strong words from such a normally quiet man. But Ella knew he was right and so she did the right thing. She went away to the girls' home to have her baby and gave it away.

The couple she decided to give it to were very impressed with Ella when they came down from New York City to meet her. They loved her cheerful disposition. So, they invited her to New York to have it. She wondered why they were being so nice to her but then she realized why. Of course, they were being nice; they were taking her child and *should* have been nice.

They told her she could stay on to breastfeed but the milk dried up a few weeks after. She had packed her bags and was waiting for them to get her a ticket home, but they postponed it for some reason. One day, she heard the baby cry and ran to it, only to see Mrs. Green standing in the nursery with Olivia in her arms, cooing at her. That image came to her often to torment her.

Ella felt so much shame at what she'd done. She never got over the image of her baby in that woman's arms. She wasn't a mother, she was just a vessel. She felt empty.

Of course, they kept asking her back to see the baby, so she would know her "biological" mother. But the real reason was because Mr. Green liked Ella. As soon as his wife would go off to sleep, he'd come into her room. She didn't sleep with him but he tried to get her to. He was a nice man, but she had sworn off having sex ever again until she got married.

"Ella," he would whisper in her ear. "You're so beautiful, so young."

"Please, Mr. Green, leave me alone."

He wouldn't. He kept at her for nearly two years, on and off, promising her love and gifts and the moon. One night, she'd had enough of trying to fight him off and said, "If you don't leave me alone, I will tell your wife."

So, he backed off. His wife's family had set him up in business and he knew that Ella could do some major damage. Not only that, he knew she would never give in.

There were two reasons Ella stopped going to New York. That was the first. It just got too complicated. Mr.

Green wasn't a bad man, he was just so lustful. He had told her she was the most beautiful woman in the world. But so had Harry Thompson. These were just words, words they thought they could use to get what they wanted. When Mr. Green realized it wasn't going to work with Ella, he stopped trying. That's when Ella realized that sex was what men wanted most. They'd say anything, promise anything to get it. But once they got it, their promises became empty and their flattering words dried up. She was done with letting any of them use her anymore. Harry Thompson had been broken-hearted when she'd told him she was going to give the baby up but now she believed he had been acting so he could have her one more time.

The second reason Ella stopped going to New York was because Olivia was growing so fast that she couldn't stand not seeing her every day. When she'd have to leave, her heart would break into a thousand pieces. She would feel like her soul was blistering with the need to be with her child. It was sheer torment. She had to get a good job and a good lawyer and then she'd get her baby back and raise it alone and to hell with what the world thought of her.

But time had passed since Ella's last visit to New York. She didn't think too much about the baby than she had to. If she thought too much, she would have gone insane. She kept working and she kept saving money to hire a lawyer and she kept praying for the day she could have Olivia back.

So, when Charlie Patterson asked her out on a date, she declined. She didn't want a man, even a rich man like Charlie. She figured all men were the same and he was just one of them. Her plans for the future only included her daughter. Charlie Patterson, simply, didn't fit into her plans.

All to Himself

Charlie Patterson was an educated man and had spent time studying finance at numerous Ivy League schools. He'd traveled to Europe, spent time with people of the upper crust and lived a life of luxury, all at his father's expense. Now, however, he was on the payroll and earning his keep.

Charlie's job at Patterson Enterprises was head of development, a job his father had created for him to keep him "busy." The title sounded important but he had little actual responsibility, which suited everyone, including Charlie, just fine. Charlie had been a difficult child, stirring up trouble, drinking too much and getting kicked of those fine Ivy League schools which had cost a fortune to get him into. But, because he was the only son and heir to Patterson Enterprises, he was never brought to task on any of his misadventures. In fact, his father would rather chuckle and look the other way where Charlie was concerned. After all, boys will be boys. He wasn't lazy, per se; he just wasn't interested in the corporation or anything other than having a good time. He hadn't matured enough to care, even though he was over thirty now. In time, he'd settle down and take responsibility. But as long as his father took care of the corporation and of everything else, Charlie didn't mind sitting back and putting his feet up on his desk.

Sure, Mr. Patterson indulged Charlie, but that's what you do when a child's mother dies so early on. Perhaps Mr. Patterson felt guilty for allowing nannies and relatives to raise him. Maybe he wanted to make it up to him and give him the best life possible. He didn't know the things Charlie had been put though and Charlie, himself, had repressed them.

He had been an overweight, insecure child who needed lots of attention. He was over-indulged with gifts but not with love or affection. His needs were never met and, because he craved constant attention, he went through a string of nannies, many of which took to beating him in order to make him "toughen up." However, the abuse didn't stop there. He also got it from his cousins, who took to taunting him because of his weight problem. More than likely they taunted him over jealousy that he got anything he wanted. However, all of this, combined with the indifference from aunts and women in general, had made Charlie into a man who kept himself distanced. These things had that had happened in his youth, though buried, still tormented Charlie. He had scars on his back and on his soul from neglect and abandon. These things, these awful things, had turned Charlie's heart cold. He didn't believe in love and warmth. He believed in lust and release. He believed in keeping himself at an aloof distance and only acting up when it served his purpose. The purpose, usually, was to get his father's attention and also to make him pay for abandoning him as a child.

This was one reason why he fancied Ella. He saw in her a kind, warm, loving person who might be able to give him some of the things he'd missed out on. Ella would make up for all that abuse. He saw something in her that made him want to be a better man. He just didn't know what lengths he would go to in order to obtain it.

The first time Charlie laid eyes on her, he thought he'd died and gone to heaven. His first thought was, "This is what I've been waiting on." Everything in his life made sense and he felt he had a purpose—to marry her. Her purpose, of course, would be to love him unconditionally and to always stay beautiful. He saw himself taking responsibly and becoming a man. He saw himself being good to Ella, to their future children. He saw her glued to his side, smiling up at him at their wedding. He saw her pregnant and barefoot. He saw her in everything that he would ever do. Life was going to be so good when Ella came around and gave him a chance. In this regard, Charlie Patterson was a bit of a romantic. He didn't see things for the way they were, he saw things the way he wanted them to be.

Ella didn't see things the same way Charlie did. When he asked her out on a date, she declined, respectively. It wasn't that Charlie was a bad guy or anything like that, it was just Ella wasn't interested in dating the boss's son. In addition to that, Charlie had a reputation that preceded him and every girl in the secretarial pool had warned her of his philandering. To Ella, a cheating man was worse than no man at all. Her mother had taught her that. She had told her of men like Charlie, men who are only out to use women and then leave them. And Ella felt like she'd been used and left already by Harry Thompson, who hadn't objected too loudly when she told him what she was going to do with their baby. Maybe she was still hurt over that and couldn't trust a man just yet. Maybe Ella just wasn't interested in Charlie Patterson. It wasn't that he was unattractive, in fact, he was a good looking man, but there was something off about Charlie Patterson. She couldn't put her finger on it but whenever she was around him, she'd find that her senses would begin to prickle. It was if her intuition was warning her of something.

Besides, Ella considered herself to be a simple country girl. What would a man like Charlie Patterson, someone who had traveled the world and been entertained by European royalty, want with a simple country girl?

Ella's refusal to go out with him drove Charlie mad. No girl had ever turned him down for a date. He was tall, attractive and he'd had his fair share of women. He was also the boss's son. That, in and of itself, should warrant a few dates.

He didn't realize Ella didn't operate like that. She was naïve and that meant she did as she chose and she chose not to start a relationship with him. She was flattered that he'd asked her out, but flattery didn't get him anywhere with

Ella. Mainly because she *was* a simple country girl at heart and she could see through just about anything. Her father had taught her that, had told her to always be a little bit suspicious of anyone "blowing smoke up your ass." And that's what she thought Charlie was doing. She didn't realize how crazy she drove him, or that he was developing an intense obsessive love for her.

And she did drive him crazy. She was so bubbly and everyone liked her. He didn't like that. He wanted her all to himself. All of her smiles should be reserved for him alone. It irked him that all the single guys in the office went after her with abandon. But he liked the fact that she turned down every single one of them. He foolishly thought she was "saving" herself for someone special and, even more foolishly, thought that someone special was him.

He tried several ways to get her to notice him. He ignored her, which didn't work. He then tried pausing in front of her desk and smiling at her. She would return his smile and go right back to her typing. He had a lot of time to think about how he could woo Ella. However, nothing seemed to work with that girl. So, he just started badgering her. Every time he would see her, he'd say, "Let's go to lunch today."

"No, thanks, Charlie, I brought mine."

"How about dinner, then?" he'd ask.

"No, thanks," she'd say with a smile. "I'm just here to work. Thank you, though."

Her refusal also gained her a lot of respect from her female co-workers. No one had ever turned Charlie Patterson down before. He'd pretty much gone through the secretarial pool and a few of the factory workers, too. He was a real playboy and they loved to see him get put in his place. Payback was indeed nice, especially to a few of the girls who had actually developed feelings for Charlie, only to be dumped.

Using his last motivator, Charlie finally got Ella to go out with him by telling her this: "If you don't, I'm going to have you fired. Not only that but you won't be able to get another job in town. I'll make sure of it."

So Ella gave in. She hated giving in to him and wondered why he couldn't take the hint. But there wasn't anything she could do. She needed her job and she liked working with all the other girls. And she foolishly thought one date couldn't hurt.

Charlie was elated as if she'd gone out with him out of genuine interest rather than through his extortion. He picked her up on Friday night in his Lincoln and drove her to the best restaurant in town. Ella supposed when he ordered lobster and champagne she should have been impressed but she wasn't. The Greens' had taken her to the best restaurants in New York City. She had been nervous at first but after a while, the restaurants just became places to eat and nothing more. She'd also been to some of the best clubs and Broadway shows as well. She wasn't the backwoods hick he thought she was. In fact, she'd studied things on her own—languages and other countries, even science. She loved to read and was always checking books out at the library. Her favorite book was *The Great Gatsby.* She had an affinity to Gatsby. While she wasn't sophisticated, she was well-rounded. And she knew what she wanted and what she didn't.

Throughout the long dinner, Charlie talked incessantly, never pausing for a breath. It was a nervous chatter and he felt like a fool. Especially when she didn't respond to him in the way he had hoped.

She finally said, "Charlie, it's getting late. I need to get home."

He nodded, paid the check and they left. He drove without saying a word, wondering why this girl still didn't like him.

When he pulled up in front of her apartment, she said, "Well, it's been fun. See you," and jumped out of the car.

Charlie got out and followed her. "Wait a minute, Ella."

She stopped at the door and turned to him. "What is it?"

"Don't I get a good night kiss?"

Her face scrunched up involuntarily. This man was too much. He came on too strong. It was enough to make her skin crawl. She stared at him and wondered why he was so interested in her. His interest was almost overbearing. She wanted to tell him to straighten up, to get some respect for himself. He was a good looking man who walked around with his head held high and demanded respect from others. And people at work seemed to respect him, even if they did tend to keep their distance. Ella assumed it was because they feared their jobs and also because they knew that one day he would be in charge of the whole company. Whatever the reason, Charlie Patterson was a man who didn't seem like he'd grovel to anyone. But now it seemed like he was groveling to her. And, like most people, she didn't like it. There was something oddly off-putting about the way he treated her. It was too much, too soon. He was too demanding. He needed something from her and he wasn't about to take no for an answer. But she wasn't about to give him a yes.

"Or you can at least invite me in for a cup of coffee," he said.

"I don't drink coffee, Charlie."

His face went red with embarrassment and he hung his head in shame over his persistence. He muttered, without looking at her, "Why don't you like me, Ella?"

Ella felt bad for Charlie. Maybe he wasn't *that* bad. Maybe she should invite him in. They could be friends but no more than that. "Come in then," she said and opened the door. "But you have to leave soon. We can't have visitors after ten."

"Okay," he said and followed her in, taking in the small but nice apartment. "Nice place."

"Yeah, it is," she said. "I don't have coffee, so what do you want to drink?"

"Got a beer?"

"No," she said. "I don't drink that much."

"Glass of water, then?" he asked.

"Sure," she said and went into the kitchen and brought him a glass of water.

He took it and said, "Thanks."

"You're welcome," she replied and sat down on the couch. "You can sit down, if you like."

He nodded and sat down, holding the glass. "So, Ella, do you like working at Patterson?"

"It's okay," she said.

"What do you plan to do?"

"What do you mean?"

"I mean," he said and stared into the glass. "Do you plan to get married or anything?"

"No," she said.

"Why not?"

"I haven't met anyone I want to marry," she said and yawned.

Those words stung Charlie and a spark of anger fired up inside him. He was someone, wasn't he? Even so, he said, "You know, if you were nice to me, I could make sure you have an easy life."

"How's that?"

"Ella," he said and set the glass down. "I'm going to level with you, okay? I like you a lot. You and I would make a great couple. I want to settle down soon and I want to settle down with a girl like you. You're the kind of girl I want to marry."

Ella stared at him in astonishment. He was already talking about marrying her? This was their first date! She stammered, "Uh, Charlie…I…uh… Look, you got the wrong girl."

"No, I got the right girl," he said. "And you're her."

She stared at him for a moment before shaking her head. "Uh, no, I'm not, Charlie. Listen, I'm tired and I want to go to bed. I don't mean to be rude, but you should leave now."

He started towards the door but stopped and asked, "Can we talk about this later?"

"No," she said and decided to set him straight. "There's nothing to talk about, Charlie. I'm sorry, but I just don't feel that way about you. I'm sure you're a nice person and all, but I'm not ready to marry or anything like that just yet."

For some reason, Charlie had thought he could convince her to give him another try. But it was obvious that he couldn't. This infuriated him, to have this little nobody treating him like *he* was nobody. He wanted to be good to her, didn't she see that?

"Ella," he said, feeling like a fool. "I just… I just want you to know that I…uh… I want you."

"But you can't have me," she said and went to the door and opened it. "And you need to leave."

He stared at her, at the door, escorting him out her life. The anger he had felt earlier grew stronger and, without thinking, he walked over and shut the door. This girl needed to know her place and be put in it. You don't treat someone like Charlie Patterson like this and get away with it. He told her, "I'm not going anywhere."

Ella's eyes widened and she wondered what he meant. He was starting to act strange. She pushed him away and told him if he didn't leave, she'd call the police.

He leaned on the door and said, "Oh, do you think they'll come and rescue you?"

She got chills from his question and backed away from him. "Charlie, you need to get a hold of yourself. You're acting strange."

"I'm strange, am I?" he asked. "What does that make you? Oh, I know what you are. You're hillbilly white trash, that's what you are. But you think for some reason that you're better than I am."

"I don't, honestly, I don't," she said and kept backing away from him. She was almost to the back wall. She held her hand up behind her to keep from colliding with it.

"Sure you don't," he said, advancing on her. "You know what else you are, Ella? You're what they call a cock-tease, that's what you are. You prance around and make men want you but you don't give it up."

"Charlie," she said, looking around for an escape. "You really need to stop. You're getting out of control."

"I've got control," he said and stopped in front of her and grabbed her arm.

"Let me go!" she hissed. "I'm warning you."

"No."

Ella glared at him, becoming angry. She grabbed a vase off the table and tried to smash it over his head. He ducked and it fell to the floor and shattered. She began to plead with him, to reason, "Charlie, stop acting like this! You don't know what you're doing."

He moved in closer and twisted her arm behind her back. "Just give me a kiss, Ella. One kiss and I'll leave."

"No!" she screamed and tried to get free of him. "Let me go, you son of a bitch!"

Charlie stared at her. Her face was red, angry. He told himself to get a grip and to stop but he couldn't, for some reason. The rejection she'd given him was hard to take and he wanted to kiss her, to show her what a good kisser he was. He wanted to give her himself, even if he had to force it on her.

"I'm warning you, Charlie," she said. "Move!"

He didn't move, not one inch. In fact, he pressed in closer to her. "I just want a kiss, that's all I want."

"Stop it!" she screamed as he tried to kiss her.

"Shh," he said and held her face in his hands and kissed her. After he was done he said, "That wasn't so bad, was it?"

It was. It was bad. It was bad because he was forcing it on her and she hated that. She hated the thought of him doing something like that to her. She had pride and he was trying to get to her. She couldn't let him. She had to stop him in his tracks and let him know this wasn't going to work. So, she spit in his face. She was almost ashamed after she did it and almost immediately regretted it. The look in his face was murderous.

"You whore," he hissed and threw her down on the floor. "How dare *you* spit on *me*?!"

"Oh, God!" she screamed and crawled away from him. He grabbed her leg, but she kicked at him. He let go and she got up and ran into the bedroom and to the window, trying to get it open. He came in and wrestled her to the bed. He knew all he had to do was to push her down, climb on top of her and there he was, in control. He ignored the horrified look on her face. He ignored her pleading, her begging. He ignored all reason, the reason at that back of his mind that told him to stop.

She pushed at him and asked, "What are you doing?"

He didn't respond. He was too lost in it to respond, even when she clawed at his face. He couldn't help himself and pathetically tried to kiss her again, which made her even more rigid.

She cried softly, "What are you doing? Stop it, Charlie."

But he couldn't stop it. Something had taken him over. And he had to make her see him. He had to force himself on her, into her. He didn't know what he was doing. She kept pushing at him, crying and begging for him to get off. But he wasn't about to. He knew he was acting like an animal but for some reason, he wanted to give himself to her, even if that meant he had to make her take it. She would realize that she brought it out and she would know he was sorry that it had come to this but it was just inside him. He had no idea it was there before now.

He ripped her dress off and raped her. He knew exactly what he was doing but he could not stop for the life of him. He knew it was wrong, that after this there was no turning back. He had never done anything like this or even thought about it. But she brought something out in him that made him do it. Something inside of him just took over.

Ella suddenly became still. She stopped moving, stopped pleading. Her head turned to the side and she stared at the wall. Tears streamed from her eyes but she didn't whimper once. It was as if she was having an out of body experience and was watching it from above. She detached herself to live through it.

Charlie knew he had to stop. He had to stop! He had to stop! He couldn't stop. He might have stopped if someone had knocked on the door. But the fact of the matter was, it would have taken an army to pull him from her.

He finished and fell off her. She curled into a ball and rolled away from him. She was sobbing, her little body shaking as she cried.

Charlie stared at her and wondered what he'd just done. Why had he done it? He couldn't think of a reason. It wasn't about sex, he knew that much. But what it was about was beyond him. He felt a wave of remorse course through his body then and he almost fell over from it. He couldn't look at her, not just yet, maybe not ever. He peeked over at her. She looked so small and helpless. What a monster he was to do that to her. He found himself speaking, the words tumbling out of his mouth with no control, "Oh, God, Ella, I'm so sorry. I don't know what came over me. I—"

"Get out!" she screamed and came up off the bed. "Get out of here!"

"Ella," he said and tried to touch her.

She jerked away and glared at him. "Get out! Now, Charlie, get out! And don't you ever come back!"

He stared at her and nodded. And then he left. As soon as she heard the front door shut, she fell back to the bed.

Of course, she didn't report it. Back then, girls didn't report things like that. People would say things like, "She brought it on herself by wearing that dress, by looking pretty, by being in the wrong place at the wrong time, by inviting him inside her apartment." They'd all be wrong, of course, but that's what the pious bastards would say anyway.

A rap came on the front door. Ella jumped up, terrified it was Charlie coming back.

"Ella?" Miss Sinclair shouted. "I was walking by and I heard something! Are you okay? Ella? Answer me!"

She wiped the tears from her face and walked into the living room and called back, "Yeah, I'm fine! I just tripped over the table. You go back to bed now."

"Alright, dear," she said and moved away from the door.

Ella cried all night, then went into a deep sleep. The next morning, she awoke and took a long bath, then went out to do her grocery shopping. When she came back, Charlie was sitting in her living room. She was startled, then she got mad. *Who the hell did this son of a bitch think he was?*

"What are you doing here?" she snapped.

"Your landlady let me in," he said. "I told her I wanted to see you."

Ella eyed him and knew he was lying. Miss Sinclair wouldn't let any strange man into one of her "girls'" apartments. She'd have made him wait outside. Ella knew he'd broken in. It wouldn't be a great accomplishment considering that the lock on the front door was flimsy. But knowing he could come in at any time horrified her. Great, now she'd have to spend money for a new lock.

"I brought you something," he said and held out a box of chocolates and a bouquet of flowers.

Ella almost fell over. He had a lot of nerve.

"So, are you okay?" he asked.

Ella wanted to scream at him, to hit him, to hurt him like he'd hurt her. But he was a man and was much larger than she was, so all she could do was ignore him. That's what she did and carried her groceries into the kitchen and set them on the counter. What the hell was going on here? What was wrong with this man? Did he not know what he'd just done?

He came into the kitchen and said, "I just want you to know I'm sorry."

She couldn't take it anymore and wheeled around and spat, "Sorry?! After what you did to me? You raped me! 'Sorry' don't cut it!"

"I am sorry, though," he said. "Let me make it up to you."

"Are you crazy or something?" she asked.

"Ella," he said, hating himself as he thought about what he had done. "I never meant to hurt you and I hate that I did. I'm not a bad person. I don't usually do stuff like that."

"Seems to me that you do," she said.

He looked away from her, feeling frustrated. Why couldn't he just walk out the door and leave and forget about her? He'd tried that, tried so hard to forget about her. But he couldn't. She'd been on his mind from the minute he'd laid eyes on her. And she'd been under his skin. That's why he was going crazy. Unrequited love will do that sort of thing.

"I just don't know who the hell you think you are," she said. "I could have you thrown in jail."

"You can't do anything," he told her.

"I can go to the police," she said. "What you did was wrong."

"Ha!" he scoffed. "Do you think for a minute that they would do anything? My old man runs this town. You don't know who you're dealing with."

"I think they call your kind rapists, Charlie," she said. "*That's* who I'm dealing with."

Her words cut into him like fire. She was doing it again. She was pushing him, pushing his buttons. He told himself to leave and to never look back. Instead he said, "Shut up. You don't know anything."

"That may be true, Charlie," she said. "But I do know that there's something wrong with you. You got a screw loose somewhere."

Before he even knew what he was doing, he backhanded her.

Ella's temple throbbed but she didn't take her eyes off him. "No real man ever hits a woman."

"Hell, I bet your daddy beat your mama every day," he said.

"He's never laid a hand on her," she hissed. "Don't you dare talk about my daddy like that! He's a good man! You're not good enough to shine his shoes!"

"Yeah, right," he said. "You're just trash, Ella, pure hillbilly white trash."

"Is that why you want me so bad?" she asked. "Yeah, I guess it is. But you can't stand the fact that I don't want you and I never will—never! That's why you keep coming back, ain't it? You can't stand that I don't want you and you get off on it. You think you can wear me down but I'm here to tell you can't. I would rather die than give in to you."

"What?" he asked, flabbergasted.

"I don't want you, Charlie. I never have and I never will."

"You'll change your mind," he said and went to the door. "One day you will want me and maybe that day I won't want *you*."

"Over my dead body," she hissed.

"So be it," he said and stepped out the door. "When you calm down I'll come back." Then he disappeared.

Ella muttered, "And I'll be ready for you."

This Poor Girl

Charlie didn't bother Ella for a few weeks after that. But it didn't matter. Her mind was on other things. She'd been throwing up every morning for two straight weeks, which meant she was most likely pregnant. But her last pregnancy hadn't been like this. *Her last pregnancy...* She wanted to cry. How could this have happened to her? She didn't ask for it. She was a good girl who was just trying to make it.

Ella went into work but couldn't concentrate. She had to type the same page four times before getting it right.

"You okay?"

Ella looked up from her work to see Jean. She smiled a little and said, "I think I'm getting sick."

"Oh, I'm sorry," Jean said and sat on the edge of Ella's desk. She leaned down and whispered, "Something's going on. Charlie didn't show up to work again today and no one knows why."

Ella knew why. He'd been staying out of work for a while now, since their "date." It was just as well. If Charlie had come near her, she might have attacked him.

"He's not still bothering you, is he?" Jean asked.

"No," Ella lied. "I mean...*no.*"

"Well, you gave him one date," Jean said, then lowered her voice, "And that's more than the bastard deserves."

Ella blanched.

"Want to go to lunch?" she asked and straightened back up.

"No thanks," Ella said. "I brought mine. I want to leave early so I'm going to work through lunch."

Jean smiled and nodded. "How about a movie tonight?"

Ella smiled back. Yeah, a movie would be good. It would take her mind off her troubles. "Sure, that sounds good."

"I'll drop by your apartment around six," Jean said and stood to leave. "See you later."

"Bye," Ella called after her then put her head in her hands. How she'd gotten into this mess, she didn't know. And now she was pregnant with Charlie's baby, from his rape. She hated him for that.

After work, she made her way by bus to the girls' home. She tried to get over there about once a month to help out Miss Abernathy. She did it out of obligation and because of the other girls. She'd been there herself and she understood their pain and their bouts of sobbing. She could console them because she once walked in their shoes.

And now she was walking in them again.

She entered the home and went straight into the kitchen, where the cook, an older woman named Cleo, smiled at her and said, "Well, if it ain't Miss Bigshot."

"Now, now," Ella said and smiled at her. "Don't start on me."

"Have it your way, girl," she said. "But how's that job going?"

The women at the home were very proud of Ella and used her as an example. "See," they'd tell the girls. "She did it. She gave her baby up but still went on to get a good job and she has her own place. You can do that, too."

"It's great," Ella said and took off her coat. "What can I do today?"

"How about chopping some onions?" Cleo asked and handed her a big bowl.

"Sure," Ella said and got to work.

"Oh, Miss Abernathy wanted you to stop by and see her as soon as you got here. I forgot to tell you."

Ella nodded. "Want me to finish the onions up first?"

"I'd love that, dear," she said with a smile.

Unfortunately, the onions were very yellow and a bit green and soon Ella's eyes were stinging and tearing. "God, these onions are awful!" she said and wiped her eyes with the back of her hand, which made it even worse.

Cleo stared at her and started laughing. Ella stared back and grumbled to herself, then she shook her head and started laughing, too. Soon, they were both laughing so hard, Cleo was doubling over and Ella eyes were watering even more. She laughed so hard, her stomach began to hurt. Life was sometimes so awful, it was funny. It seems she had to laugh to keep from crying.

"Girl," Cleo laughed. "You look like you just lost best friend."

"I did—you!" Ella said and laughed. "I'm never helping you again! I knew I shouldn't have come in here first."

"But you love the kitchen the best."

Ella stopped laughing and thought about that. She did love the kitchen the best. It was where all the girls would come in and talk, snacking on the cookies and little cakes Cleo always made for them. Ella remembered being back at home with her mother, helping her in the kitchen, how they would talk and laugh as they prepared the meals for the family. Her mother would tell her stories of her own childhood, how her daddy had taught her to make moonshine, much to her mother's chagrin. About how she was a tomboy and loved to climb trees better than anything. Ella would tell her mother about her big plans for the future and her mother would always say, "Oh, Ella, why won't you stay here with me a little longer? I love having you home. Stay another year and we'll see about sending you to college."

But she didn't get to go to college. She had a baby instead. On a recent visit, her mother asked when she might get married and warned her that everyone in Cumberland Gap thought she ran the risk of becoming an old maid. She knew they called her "mommy's girl", but she didn't care because being mommy's girl was what she liked best. But she knew she was no longer mommy's girl. She felt her heart ache for that time and she burst into tears.

"Lord, girl, what's gotten into you?" Cleo said. "I didn't mean nothing by that!"

"Oh, I know, Cleo. I ain't crying cause of... It's nothing," Ella said, then lied, "It's just my job, it's so hard. I was just thinking about it, that's all."

Cleo came over and hugged her. "Shh, now, shh."

Just then, Miss Abernathy came in saying, "Ella, I've been looking all over for you." She stopped abruptly when she saw Cleo consoling her. "What's going on in here?"

"Onions," Cleo said and pulled away from Ella. "She's crying over them old onions."

Ella laughed a little.

"Humm..." Miss Abernathy muttered. "Ella, would you mind coming into my office? I need to talk to you about something."

"Sure," Ella said and followed her into the office. She sat down in one of the chairs and wiped at her eyes. "What can I do for you, Miss Abernathy?"

Miss Abernathy sat at her desk and said, "It's nothing really. It's just we're going to be getting a new girl and you know how I like you to talk to the new girls at first."

Ella nodded.

"But I was thinking," she said. "You know how sad they are when they first come in? Well, I was thinking about maybe throwing a little party to welcome them in. That way, they can mingle with the other girls and start making friends right off."

"That's a wonderful idea," Ella said and stared out the window. It was winter again and the outside looked so cold and uninviting.

"And, I was thinking that we could perhaps give them a little welcome gift, too," she went on, though Ella wasn't listening. "I was thinking something small but something they could take with them when they leave. Like a nice brush and comb set."

Ella stared at the trees. All the leaves were gone and they looked bare and lonely. She had always noticed the changing of the seasons back home and it seemed like a bigger deal then than it did now. She and her two sisters would go into the woods and collect kindling for the fire. They would throw leaves and chase each other, laughing and yelling, "I'm telling Mommy!" She missed Susie and Irene with a vengeance.

"Ella?" Miss Abernathy said, jarring her out of her memories.

"Yes?" she said and sat up taller.

Miss Abernathy eyed her and said, "What's wrong?"

"Nothing," Ella said. "Just tired from work."

"Do you need to lie down for a while?"

"No," Ella replied, shaking her head.

Miss Abernathy got up and came around the desk and sat in the other chair. She forced Ella to look at her and said, "I know something's wrong, now you tell me."

Ella stared into her kind eyes for a moment before bursting into tears. "I can't."

"What's wrong?"

"Nothing," Ella cried.

"Tell me."

Ella wiped the tears off her face and stared around the room. "I did it again. Well, I didn't do it, it was done to me, Miss Abernathy. I swore it wouldn't happen again and it has. But I didn't ask for it, I swear I didn't."

Miss Abernathy knew exactly what she meant and a spark of anger fired up in her belly. She was a veteran of things like this, and knew exactly what Ella was talking about. She felt a hate for men—all men—so strong then she could have spit. And Miss Abernathy never spit, she was too lady-like. She, herself, had been down this road before. That might be the reason she never married or had anything to do with men. The only men she talked to were those that came to do handy-man jobs around the home.

"Shh," Miss Abernathy said and pulled her into her arms. "Shh, Ella."

Ella allowed herself to be held, to be consoled. She sobbed, "What can I do now? I can't have this baby. It will kill my daddy. It will kill him!"

"Shh…"

"Men are such bastards!" Ella shouted, sitting up and shaking her head. "I hate them! I hate all of them! All they do is use us and hurt us! My daddy is the only decent man on this earth! And it would kill him. If I told him I was having another baby like this, it would kill him. And I didn't even…" She stopped and stared into space. "Nothing."

Miss Abernathy stared at her thinking, *This poor girl. This poor, poor girl.* She took out her handkerchief from her pocket and handed it to Ella. "Wipe your face, honey."

Ella took the handkerchief and wiped her face and watched Miss Abernathy get up and go to a little medicine cabinet where she kept all the aspirins and other medical supplies. She rummaged around for a while, reaching deeply into it and pulled out a bottle. She brought it back over to Ella.

"What's that?" Ella asked.

"It's…" Miss Abernathy stopped and stared intensely at Ella. "It's… It can help you, Ella."

Ella stared at her, wondering what she meant. "What does it do?"

"It will bring your period on."

Ella wondered what that meant, then she got it. She breathed a sigh of relief. She grabbed at the bottle greedily but Miss Abernathy held it out of her reach.

"Ella, are you sure you want to do this?"

"Of course," she said. "I *have* to do it."

"Whose baby is it?"

Ella clamped her mouth shut. That was none of her business. She didn't want anyone to know what Charlie Patterson had done to her. She didn't even like to think about it herself.

"I won't tell anyone," she said. "I promise."

"I can't tell you," Ella said. "Sorry."

"You don't want to press charges?"

Ella laughed thinking about what Charlie had said. "I don't think that would be in my best interest, Miss Abernathy."

Miss Abernathy nodded and said, "So you want to do this, do you?"

"I do."

"Now you know this is going to hurt, don't you?"

"I don't care," she said. "Give it to me."

"Honey, listen to me," she said and forced her to look in her eyes. "It's going to hurt a lot, probably more than childbirth."

Ella shrugged. She'd take the pain, anything was better than this, than having Charlie Patterson's rape baby.

Miss Abernathy reluctantly handed her the bottle. "I'll go get your coat and purse. You need to go home and think about this."

Ella nodded and held the bottle tightly. This was her salvation. She trusted Miss Abernathy with her life. She knew she'd help her.

"Be right back," Miss Abernathy said and left the room.

Ella watched her go, then stared at the bottle. She had an urge so strong to untwist the cap and drink it all that she almost did it. In that bottle was the only way out of her predicament. In a few minutes, Miss Abernathy came back into the room and helped her into her coat. Ella put the bottle into her purse and snapped it shut.

"You go home now," Miss Abernathy said. "You go home and rest and decide what you want to do. You call me once you decide, too. Don't take this lightly, Ella. Don't take it lightly."

"I won't," she promised. "Thank you, Miss Abernathy."

Ella went home and immediately drank the medicine down, ignoring Miss Abernathy's request for a call. She wanted make sure Miss Abernathy wouldn't talk her out of doing it. She'd made her decision and she would follow through with it, no matter what. The medicine tasted awful and she had to drink two glasses of water afterwards to get the bitter taste out of her mouth. She stared at the bottle. It was still half-full. *Would that be enough?* She assumed so and decided to take the rest back to Miss Abernathy. So, she put it back in her purse and wondered when it would work.

She stood at the kitchen sink for a little while watching the neighborhood kids kicking a ball in the street. She was about to yell at them to get out of the street, they'd almost been run over just last week, but she suddenly felt woozy.

"Oh," she said and held her head, which was now spinning. That stuff must really work and it must work quickly. Ella steadied herself and tried to take a step but her legs suddenly gave out from under her and she fell to the floor.

The world seemed so far away then and her mind began to visualize things, intense things, intense colors. Was she hallucinating? She wasn't sure but she seemed to be floating. It wasn't so bad for a while, it was like she was intoxicated, the way she felt when she'd drank too much moonshine. Moonshine... She smiled to herself with the memory of sneaking a jar out of the house and to Harry Thompson, who was waiting on her by the riverbank.

"Told ya I'd get it," she'd said and handed it to him.

"Damn, Ella!" he'd exclaimed. "Your mama will be madder than a wet hen if she finds out."

"Then let's drink it all," she said and nuzzled his neck, breathing in his masculine scent. "Oh, Harry, you smell so good today."

He'd kissed her then, kissed her lightly and softly, taking her away the way he always did. Harry had been an awfully good kisser, that was one thing you could say about that boy. And he'd charm the pants off a snake. Harry... Harry and the moonshine, the day at the riverbank, the sun shining and everything peaceful and right with the world as he held her close and whispered how much he loved her, how he was going to do the right thing by her. All lies, but nice to hear, nonetheless.

She continued to think about that day with Harry but all of a sudden, she felt a cramp in her stomach and doubled over with it, screaming as she held it. *Was she dying?* What was happening? How quickly the feeling had gone from euphoria to pain, the way love does. How quickly the good feeling left her, just like that first love feeling had left. It seemed so long ago that it didn't feel like part of her anymore, that feeling of love. It felt like the love belonged to someone else and she'd only witnessed it, or read about it in a book. It wasn't hers anymore, it was just gone and it was distant, the only thing she felt from it was the empty space it had left in her heart.

"I love you, Ella," Harry said and stared into her eyes. "I love you so damn much it hurts me."

Her stomach was hurting her now. She was beginning to go into a downward spiral. She knew she needed to get to the phone and she needed help. She wished she hadn't been stubborn and had called Miss Abernathy but there was nothing she could do about that now. She just hadn't realized how badly it would hurt. But she knew she had to call someone. She didn't know who, but she'd call someone. She wanted to call her mother, so bad. But that was the last person she wanted to bother with this. For an instant, she wished she *could* call her mother, she wished she was home, in her arms, being consoled.

"Ella, Ella, Ella," her mother had murmured in her ear. "Oh, girl, what have you gone and gotten yourself into?"

"Mommy, I'm so sorry," she cried. "It's just—"

"He talked you into it, didn't he?" she asked and kissed her cheek. "It's okay, honey. I'll talk to your daddy and we'll figure this thing out. Don't you worry none now. We'll get it fixed and no one will ever have to know."

The image and feeling of being in her mother's arms left her and Ella seemed to jerk awake. Had she fallen asleep? She shook her head and got up on her elbows and dragged herself towards the phone. Then she passed out for a moment. She came to again and shook her head and tried again. She got about two feet before she collapsed.

She laid there for a long time, feeling the convulsions. But they didn't hurt. She was in so much pain, her body had gone into shock. After a few more minutes, she gave into the unconsciousness which was determined to take her over.

Sign of Life

It was right at six when Jean knocked on Ella's door. She waited for a minute or so, then knocked again. "Come on, Ella!" she called. "We're going to be late!"

She waited for a minute but then decided that Ella might be taking a bath or something. She tried the door, it was unlocked, so she went in, smiling and said cheerily, "It's time for the movie! Ella?"

Ella didn't answer. Jean looked around and then walked into the kitchen and found her collapsed in the middle of the floor. She screamed, "Ella!"

She got down beside her and slapped her face but she wasn't coming to. Then she noticed all the blood. Ella's skirt was soaked in blood.

"Oh, God," she muttered. "Oh, God, Ella, what have you done?"

She looked around, wondering what the next step was. She looked back at Ella and knew immediately what she had done to herself. She panicked for a minute, not knowing what to do. She'd never felt more powerless in her entire life. If she took her to a hospital, she might get in trouble, but she couldn't leave her lying on the floor much longer. Ella was going to die soon if Jean didn't get it together.

Her eyes settled on the phone and she wondered if she could do it. She wondered if she could call him and ask for his help. She didn't have much choice. She got up and picked up the phone and called him. She knew him as Jack, everyone else knew him as Dr. Williams. She hadn't seen him in over a year but she knew his office number by heart and knew he'd be working late. He picked up on the third ring.

"It's me and don't hang up," she said. "If you don't want your wife to find out about us, you come over here right now. I need your help."

And he did. Once he got there, he immediately went to Ella and dropped down beside her. "Let's get her into bed," he said.

They picked her up and took her into the bedroom and laid her down. That's when he started trying to wake her up. It took him over fifteen minutes to get a sign of life out of her.

Ella awoke to find a strange man slapping her face. She focused on him, then over his shoulder at Jean, who was standing in the doorway of her bedroom looking very anxious. She'd forgotten that they were supposed to go to the movies.

"Wake up, girl," Jack said. "Good, you hear me? No, no, wake up, girl."

Ella tried to regain consciousness but it was so hard not to go back to sleep.

"What did you take, girl?" he said. "Tell me what you took. What did you take to get rid of that baby? Come on, now, tell me what you took."

Ella stared at him. How did he know about the baby? He looked so blurry. He slapped her face again.

"Don't go to sleep, girl," he said. "That's the worst thing you can do right now. Wake up!" He looked over his shoulder. "Jean, go get me some ice cold water right now."

Jean jumped and ran off. Ella almost fell over. He set her up straight again. "Tell me what you took. Come on, girl, tell me."

"Purse...in...purse..." Ella muttered.

"Get her purse!" he yelled. When Jean came back in a minute later with the water and purse, he said, "Pour that water in her face. Now!"

He grabbed the purse and tore through it, finding the little bottle almost immediately. He uncapped it and sniffed, ascertained it was some type of herbal concoction, the kind that if mixed wrong, could lead to what Ella was now going through. *The things people would do to themselves just because they don't think there's any other way out...* He knew she probably didn't have any other choice but the fact that she *had* to do this to herself enraged him. He was so enraged, he threw the bottle up against the wall in a fury. He stared at Ella. If she'd only come to him... Well, he couldn't have helped her and that made him angrier. But maybe he could have done something so she wouldn't be on her death bed. Maybe he could have talked her out of it, told her what would happen to her. However, there was nothing he could do about that right now. Right now he had to help her, had to keep her alive.

He and Jean stayed up all night with Ella, keeping her awake and keeping her temperature down. At dawn, it was safe to let her go to sleep. But then Ella began to talk in her sleep, "Didn't want him. Didn't love him."

"What's she talking about?" Jack asked Jean, who shrugged.

Ella kept on, "Go away and leave me alone, go away...you...go...away. *Now!*"

She rose up in the bed and pointed at Jack, who felt her icy stare so much it sent chills down his spine. He and Jean raced over to her. They pushed her back down and got her calm.

"What's wrong with her?" Jean asked.

"She's hallucinating," he told her.

Jena nodded and they stayed by her side for a few more hours, then Jack told her that he had to leave. Jean walked him to the door.

"You did a good thing," Jean told him.

He nodded. "If you ever need...*that*, don't you dare take that stuff. You come to me, alright?"

She nodded.

"Bye, Jean," he said and started out the door, then stopped. "You take care now."

"You too," Jean muttered.

Then he left and she went back into the bedroom where Ella was still talking in her sleep, moaning about someone leaving her alone. Jean knew who she was talking about and had to put her hands over her ears to stop it from driving her crazy. *That bastard Charlie Patterson!*

When Ella finally woke hours later the first thing she said was, "Don't tell anyone."

"I won't," Jean said and took her hand, squeezing it. "It's over now."

"No," Ella said. "I think it's just getting started."

Ella swore this was never going to happen to her again. And she was right. Dr. Williams insisted she come in for a check-up, then called her a few days later, telling her that she'd probably lost her ability to have children as there had been some scarring occur. It was a side effect of the stuff that she had taken.

Ella was numb. What did she ever do to deserve this? It wasn't right, it just wasn't fair. She stared at the phone and rushed over to it, calling Lawson's Grocery. When Mr. Lawson picked up, she said sweetly, "Mr. Lawson, it's Ella."

"Ella!" he exclaimed. "How are you, girl?"

"Good," she said. "I need to talk to my mommy."

"Oh, hold on," he said. "I swear she just left. Let me go get her."

Ella smiled and when her mother came on the phone a few minutes later, her smile deepened. "Mommy!"

"Girl," Ruth said. "I was just thinking about you—swear to the good Lord above."

"How are the girls?" she said. "And the twins? And Daddy? How is Daddy doing?"

"Fine and good," she replied. "We all miss you a bunch."

"I miss you too," Ella said. "I wish I could come home more."

"I wish you could, too," she said. "Want me to send you some money?"

"Oh, no," she said. "I know you can't afford it. I'll be up in a month or so, I promise."

"Well, if you promise," Ruth teased. "But I have a few extra dollars if you need it…"

"No, thanks, Mommy," Ella said.

"Sure?"

"Yes, I'm sure. Listen, Mommy," Ella said. "I was… Uh… Daddy's gun, that old pistol, I want it."

Her mother was immediately suspicious. "Why do you need a gun?"

"For protection," she said quickly, trying to think of an excuse, then going for the most obvious. "Knoxville's a big place, Mommy. All kinds of different people around. You never know who you can trust."

"What are you talking about, Ella?" she asked. "Did someone hurt you or something?"

"No," she said and pretended to scoff. "I would just feel safer with a gun. Can Daddy send me that old pistol?"

"I'll see about it," she said. "Are you sure everything's okay? You can tell me anything, I'm your mother."

"It's fine," Ella reassured her. "Everything is fine. Can you send the gun or not?"

"I can," she said.

Ella smiled. "Thanks, Mommy."

The gun came a few days later. Ella opened it up and pulled it out. Just holding it in her hands made her feel better. She felt so much safer with that gun in her possession but that wasn't the real reason she wanted it. She knew the only thing that would stop Charlie Patterson was a bullet. And she planned on using one on him.

If Doc had known all this, he would have put a bullet in Charlie Patterson himself. But Ella didn't tell anyone. Besides, she wanted the pleasure of doing it herself.

One Warning

"I heard you were sick," Charlie said at the door, holding up flowers. "Can I come in?"

"Yeah, come in, Charlie," Ella said and even smiled at him.

He wondered about her smile, but shrugged it off. Maybe she was beginning to like him. He was a good guy, he really was. He just wasn't good around Ella.

"So, what happened?" he asked as he settled on the couch.

"What do you mean?"

"They were saying you were sick at work," he said. "You've been out a week."

Ella stared at him, looking innocent. "Just a cold."

"Oh," he said. "Well, you're better now, right?"

Ella ignored his question and asked, "What are you doing here?"

"Well," he said. "I wanted to see how you were. I care about you, Ella."

"That so?" she asked and headed to the bedroom. "Excuse me for a minute, Charlie."

He nodded and waited on her. He was really nervous but she was acting a lot nicer. He was going to make up for the bad things he'd done to her. He reached into his pocket and pulled out an envelope stuffed with money.

Ella came back out a minute later, hiding the gun behind her back. She started to speak, but Charlie held up his hand for her to listen.

"I've been thinking," he said. "We got off on the wrong foot and I want to make it up to you."

"Umm…" Ella said, as if she was considering.

"I don't know what came over me," he said. "But I am so sorry, Ella. I hate myself for what I did to you and I want to do something to fix it."

Ella eyed him, then eyed the envelope. "What's that?"

"Money," he said. He had gotten out of a lot of trouble with money. He was confident that it would serve him well in this situation, too. "Take the money, Ella. Let me make up for it."

But this wasn't a situation that could be remedied with money. He ought to know that, Ella thought. She wondered if that boy had a lick of sense. He just didn't get it, did he?

"I…I just hate what I did," he said and paused, taking a breath. He continued, desperately trying to get his point across, "Please let me apologize and let me make it up to you. I don't know what came over me and I am just so sorry, Ella. I want us to be together and I want to make it up to you. Please take this money and let's start fresh."

"I don't want your money," she said.

"Well, I don't want it either," he said and threw it down on the coffee table.

"You know what I want, Charlie?" she asked. "I want you to feel a little bit of what I felt. Can you do that for me?"

"I will," he said, nodding, not really knowing where she was going.

"Sure?" she said. "It might hurt."

"I'll take a bullet if I have to."

She smiled. "I'm glad you said that, Charlie."

His eyes narrowed. He'd meant it figuratively, of course.

"Ready or not, here I come," she said and pulled the gun out. She pointed the gun at him and fired, hitting her intended target—his foot. The room filled with smoke and Charlie screamed. Once the smoke cleared, Ella almost laughed at him as he hopped up and down and cursed. He'd probably walk with a limp for the rest of his life. She got some satisfaction from that.

"What are you doing, you crazy bitch?!" he yelled.

She leveled the gun at his head. "Hold still, Charlie. Hold still for a minute."

His eyes nearly popped out of his head.

"This is a warning," she said, walking over to him. "Stop moving."

"What the hell are you doing?"

"Getting my satisfaction," she said. "Isn't that what we were talking about?"

"You're crazy," he spat. "How dare you shoot me?"

"You said I could," she said and pointed the gun at his head. He stopped moving and stared at the gun. "This is it, Charlie. No more after this. No more Charlie coming over here. No more Charlie asking me out. No more Charlie pushing himself on me. No more Charlie, period."

He stood stock still and braced himself.

Ella chuckled to herself and lowered the gun. "I see I got my point across."

Charlie breathed a sigh of relief but said, "You're a crazy bitch."

"And this crazy bitch is done with you," she said. "One warning and that's all you get. If you *ever* cross my door again, the next bullet from this gun goes in your head."

"Why are you doing this?" he asked, almost wailing with pain.

"Cause you asked for it," she said. "And I mean it. Remember, I'm nothing but a white trash hillbilly, Charlie. That means I'm crazy and I don't need a reason to fire *my* gun. Think long and hard about that before you come back here again."

"You bitch!" he roared, hating her. "What am I going to tell everyone?"

"You'll think of something, Charlie," she said, trying to hide her smile. "You could just tell them you shot yourself in the foot."

He glared at her.

"It's over," she said. "Oh, and let me say this. I don't plan on losing my job, either."

He shook his head in a rage.

"Now, I'm going to count to five. At five, I fire again and let me tell you, I'm a helluva shot. One...two...three..." She stopped. He was out the door and gone from her life. She hoped.

She smiled to herself and lowered the gun. Sometimes, a gun was the only way to talk sense into some people. She hated that it had come down to that, but it had.

Just then, Miss Sinclair rushed in. "What was that noise?"

"Oh, shoot, Miss Sinclair," Ella said. "I'm sorry. I was cleaning this old gun and it went off."

Miss Sinclair studied her, then the gun. "Girl, put that gun up and stop waving it around like that. You're going to hurt yourself."

"I will," she said sweetly.

Miss Sinclair shook her head and said, "I'm cooking supper tonight and I expect you to be there."

"Alright," Ella said gently. "I'll see you later."

"Fine," she said, eying her. "But I'm warning you about that gun. You'll hurt yourself with it."

Ella nodded and shut the door after her, then eyed the money on the coffee table. She went over and picked the envelope up. Inside was over a thousand dollars. She looked up at the ceiling. This might be enough to get Olivia back. But then she felt weird about having Charlie's money.

She got up and went to the cloth-covered box in her closet where she kept all of Olivia's pictures. She took it to the bed and sorted through it until she found the card she was looking for: Dean Bellows, Attorney at Law. It was time. She'd take that money and she'd get her baby back, then her life would be better. She knew it was hopeless but it was the only thing she had to hang onto, the hope that someday she and Olivia would be together. It was that hope that blinded her to reason. But the hope had also kept her going for so long, it served its purpose well. Besides, without hope, life isn't much fun.

The next day after work, Ella took the bus to Mr. Bellows law office. The secretary immediately recognized her and smiled widely. "Well, hello, Ella. How are you?"

"Fine," she said. "And you?"

"Good," she said. "What can I do for you?"

"I'd like to see Mr. Bellows if he isn't too busy."

"Oh, I think he has an opening," she said and got up, walked over to his office door and rapped on it. She opened it a crack and said, "Ella Muroc is here to see you."

"Let her in," he called.

"Go on in, Ella," she said.

Ella nodded and went into Mr. Bellows office. He stood up from his desk and came over to give her a hug. He liked Ella very much and thought she was a wonderful young woman. She'd also brought him a lot of money but he did feel some shame for taking it—some. But of course, those people in New York had been willing to pay top dollar, so it might as well have been him rather than some other lawyer to take their money. Even so, Mr. Bellows donated a portion of the money to the girls' home, probably out of guilt. Miss Abernathy, who had been delighted at such a generous donation, invited him to a special dinner with her and her "girls." There, he and Ella had conversed. She had so impressed him, he'd told her, "If you ever need anything, let me know, Ella."

"How are you?" he asked and stood back to look at her. "You get prettier every day."

She blushed. "Thank you, Mr. Bellows."

"Sit down," he said and motioned her into a chair before he took his behind the desk. "What can I do for you?"

Ella smiled shyly and took out the money and slid it over to him. "That should be more than enough."

Mr. Bellows eyed the money. "Where did you get this?"

"Does it matter?" she asked nervously. "We can do it now."

"Do what, Ella?"

"Get my baby back," she said and smiled. "There's over a thousand dollars there."

Mr. Bellows blanched. There was no way she had enough money to get her baby back. There wasn't enough money in the world to take that baby back from the Greens'. The woman's family was one of the richest and most powerful in the entire country, probably the whole world. Mr. Bellows had been nervous around them, but they'd been nice enough. Of course, Ella didn't have any idea about things like that. And she'd been in here more than once trying to get him to do something about the situation. It was time he set her straight. The girl was ruining her life over this and she needed to move on.

"Ella," he told her gently. "We've talked about this, girl."

"There's enough money," she said.

"No, there's not," he said.

"What can I do then?" she asked in a panic. "I got the money, Mr. Bellows. Call the Greens' and tell them I want my baby back."

"I can't do that, Ella," he said. And he couldn't. If he did that, the Greens' would have a pack of lawyers beating him into the ground from the word "go."

"I'll do anything, Mr. Bellows," she said. "Anything."

"But there's nothing you can do, Ella," he said.

"You said if I had some money, we could do something," she cried.

He had but he never thought this young girl would ever get her hands on any money. He felt bad for lying to her, for giving her false hope. He eyed her, staring at her nice clothes and purse. She looked like a million bucks now but when she'd come in here for the first time, she'd been dressed in a plain calico dress, new but unflattering. He remembered how her shoes looked worn and old. But when she'd smiled, he'd overlooked everything that made a person form judgments—and misconceptions. That smile made up for the fact that she was a poor girl. It told the world she had a lot to offer, if only everyone would overlook what she wasn't born with or where she came from.

Mr. Bellows sighed, hating to set her straight, but she had to be set straight. Someone had to tell her to get on with her life and he figured it might as well be him. He took a breath and said, "I'm going to tell you what to do and if you do it, you'll get over this."

She glared at him, hating the words that were about to come out of his mouth.

"Find you a nice man," he said gently. "Get married and have another baby."

She looked away from him. Were there any nice men out there? She doubted it.

"When you have another baby," he said. "You'll get over your first."

He didn't know that she couldn't have another baby. She supposed all hope was lost.

"Take your money and go, Ella," he told her. "Take it and buy yourself something nice."

She stood and he handed her the envelope. "Bye, Mr. Bellows. I won't bother you again."

"Don't say that, Ella," he said. "I know you're hurt right now, but you will get over it."

"When?" she asked and felt tears sting her eyes. "When will I get over it?"

"Find yourself a nice man," he said again. "And you'll get over it."

She nodded and headed to the door.

"Ella," he called. "You know you're always welcome here."

"Thank you, Mr. Bellows," she said and closed the door on her way out.

Ella went home and into her bedroom and opened the closet door, taking out her suitcase. She ripped the liner out at the top and sewed the money into it, for safekeeping. She didn't think it was a good idea just leaving money like that around.

Then she went into the kitchen and took down a bottle of whiskey she had for hot-toddies. She took a swig and let the tears flow. It was really over. She'd never have Olivia back. She'd never have another baby. She'd never have anything.

The sobs overtook her and she slid down the wall and cried. She kept taking swigs from the bottle, getting drunker than she'd ever gotten. Then she fell asleep in the floor and awoke the next morning with a hangover.

A Nice Man

Frank Jones was a nice man. He was also very successful, having built an insurance agency from the ground up. He was conscious of his appearance and only dressed in the best suits. He figured if you looked successful, you'd be successful. And in his case, he was right.

The day Frank Jones showed up at Patterson Enterprises to discuss the company's insurance with the bosses, the women swooned. As he walked by their desks, he looked like a movie star—tall, dark and so handsome it hurt. Of course, when he saw Ella, he forgot about everyone else in the room. She didn't even notice him, which made him pay her even more attention. He went to his meeting and afterwards made a point of stopping at her desk to say hello. And he was ignored. But then again, maybe she just didn't hear him.

"Hello," he said again and cleared his throat.

But Ella had heard him. She'd just ignored him. In fact, when he first stopped by her desk, she had thought, *Oh, no, not another one* and wondered why men just couldn't take the hint when a girl wasn't interested.

"I'm Frank Jones," he said and extended his hand.

She ignored his hand and said, "I'm not interested."

Frank's face reddened, then he shook his head. "Oh, well then. Sorry to bother you."

Ella watched him walk away. Just then Jean stomped over to her desk and said, "What the hell are you doing?"

"What do you mean?"

She leaned down and whispered, "He's a nice man. Give him a chance."

"I'm done with men," Ella said bitterly. "I'm gonna get a cat."

Jean rolled her eyes, then snapped, "You've never had a good man, that's what's wrong with you. He's a good man. Now give him a chance."

"*You* give him a chance."

"He didn't talk to me," she said. "Now get up and go after him."

"No way."

"Fine," Jean said and started off.

Ella jumped up and ran after her, grabbing her arm. "What are you doing?"

"Giving him your number."

"You are not doing that."

"I am so," she said and wriggled out of Ella's grasp.

Ella grabbed for her again but she was gone. She stopped Frank Jones at the elevator and started talking to him. Frank looked over at Ella and smiled. She groaned and wondered what this one would do to her.

Frank took her out for dinner and dancing. She picked at her food and watched everyone else have fun on the dance-floor. However, he wasn't overbearing and didn't force her to talk. He didn't know what her problem was but he knew if he could break her hard shell, he would find a wonderful person inside. Frank knew people and he instinctively knew if they were good or bad—this is what made him a good insurance salesman. And while he wasn't interesting in selling Ella insurance, he knew she was a good one, even if she wasn't giving him a chance in hell. No matter what he did, no matter how well he treated her, Ella wasn't having it. When he dropped her off at her apartment, he got out and raced to open her door, but she already had it open and was headed up the walk.

"Well," he muttered, then called after her, "Uh, it was nice."

She threw her hand up and went to the front door, taking out her key. "Thanks, Frank."

He nodded and dropped his head. Had he done something wrong? He stared back at her and said, "Can I call you?"

She turned and gave him a hellacious look. "Are you kidding me?"

"I didn't… What do you mean?"

Ella advanced on him, her pent-up frustration was coming to a boil and she couldn't stop herself. "I'll tell you what I mean. I don't like you. No, wait a minute, I don't like men. Period. Okay? You should know that before you waste your precious time."

"I didn't think I was wasting my time," he muttered. "I'm sorry to have bothered you."

She nodded with satisfaction, glad she was finally getting through to someone. "Damn right you bothered me. Isn't that what all you men do? You go to school to learn how to drive women crazy or something?"

Frank stared at her in disbelief, wondering why he was the victim of her sharp tongue. He was there and he was a man, that's all the reason Ella needed.

"So just go, Frank Jones," she said, shaking her head. "Just get into your fancy car and find yourself a fancy girl and have fancy babies."

She turned on her heel, leaving him flabbergasted. He watched her go into the apartment and was suddenly angry himself. He hated the fact that everyone thought he had always had it easy—he hadn't. He'd been raised dirt poor and had worked for everything he had. He just didn't go around complaining about it and trying to convince everyone how hard he had it. People who did that, in his opinion, were weak. And Frank Jones was not weak. Nor did he like to get run over.

Before he could stop himself, he stomped up the walk and into the house. Then he got confused. Which door was hers? He knocked on the first one and was relieved when Ella opened it up.

"What the hell do you want?" she asked. "Didn't you get the point?"

"Let me tell you something," he said, pointing his finger in her face. "I am not 'fancy'. I've worked for everything I've got and I won't have anyone throw it up in my face."

Ella was taken aback.

Frank started to turn away, but instead said, "And another thing. Don't agree to go out with someone and then act like a child when you do. You don't have to let your host know you're not enjoying it. That's really quite immature."

"I didn't enjoy it!"

"Really?" he asked. "Like I couldn't tell that!"

"I didn't want to go out with you in the first place!"

"Then you should have said no when I called!" he yelled.

"Why? You'd keep badgering me about it."

"Girl," he said. "Look at me. Do I look like I have to badger anyone for a date?"

No, he didn't. Even so, Ella hissed, "Go to hell," and slammed the door in his face.

He nodded and started out, changed his mind and went into her apartment.

"Get out of here!" she yelled.

"Ten-ninety-eight," he said.

"What?"

"I want my money back for your dinner," he said.

"Are you crazy?"

"No," he said. "But I want my money back."

Fine," she growled and grabbed her purse. When she looked inside her empty wallet, her shoulders slumped. She was broke, again. "I don't have it."

Well, the point was lost now, wasn't it? He was just trying to get her back anyway but her being broke made him feel even worse. He didn't know what to say then, so he nodded and mumbled, "Well, then... Okay." He turned on his heel to leave the room. That's when Ella cracked up. She was laughing so hard, she was doubling over.

"You're crazy," she laughed. "You're crazier than I am."

He started laughing too. "I'm not the one jumping on people here."

She kept laughing and pointing at him. "Do you really want your money back?"

"No," he said. "I just want you to straighten up."

She laughed again, then shook her head. The seriousness was back and it crossed her face, taking away the joy she'd just felt. She realized she was sick of it, of the misery. She was sick of the big wall she'd had to build up around herself, too.

Frank stared at her and smiled. He didn't care that she'd just yelled at him nor did he care that she might not like him. Even if she'd acted awful on their date, she was still a delight to be around and he was grateful for his one opportunity. She was also very beautiful which made everything harder but made the desire to be around her stronger.

"Frank," she said and sighed. "I'm going to be straight with you. I'm not what you're looking for. I know you're a good man and I know you'd treat me good and all that, but it just ain't gonna happen. I'm sorry."

He nodded, taking the defeat well. "That's fine, Ella. All you had to do was tell me that to begin with and I wouldn't have bothered you."

Ella felt something stir inside of her. She didn't know what it was. She didn't know if it was lust or like or even love. It was just something inside of her beginning to emerge. It was a good feeling that would make way for more good feelings. The thought of being happy for once came to her and she almost backed away from it, thinking she didn't deserve to be happy, not after all she'd done. But, as she stared at Frank, she knew if she let him leave she'd regret it.

She needed a good man, she really did. So, she had to test him to see if he could handle her and the things she'd done. If he couldn't, then he could go to hell.

"I'll be leaving then," he said and turned to the door.

"Wait a minute," she said and came up behind him and shut the door. She turned to him and looked into his deep blue eyes and again felt something stir in her. It might have been hope and hope was what had been missing for so long. Her soul had been weighed down with regret and grief for too long. She was tired of feeling so old when she was still so young.

"What is it?" he asked softly.

"If I tell you something, do you promise not to hate me?"

"I'd never hate you," he said. "What is it?"

She took a breath and said, "I'm not a nice person, Frank. You need to know that."

"Yeah, you are," he said.

She backed away from him and said, "Ha! You think I'm nice? Let me ask you this and I bet it'd change your mind. Does a nice girl get pregnant out of wedlock and have a baby and then give it up?"

His mouth dropped.

"You might as well know from the start," she said and knew she was trying to drive him away but couldn't help herself. "What do you think of that? I gave my baby up. I'm evil."

"You are not evil," he said, wanting to console her. "Sometimes things just happen the way they happen, Ella, that's all. It's not because you're evil that it happened, it just happened."

"But I am evil," she said as tears streamed down her cheeks. "I know the difference between right and wrong and I've done wrong, Frank. I know that's why I'm being punished."

"How are you being punished?"

She thought of the baby she'd gotten rid of, then of Charlie. That's how. For some reason, she wanted to tell him that, too. She wanted to tell someone if only for opportunity for them to confirm that she was bad. Or maybe she wanted to be comforted, told she didn't have any other choice. She wanted someone to understand. She wanted it off her chest. If she stopped holding it in, then maybe it wouldn't torment her so much. If she could only tell someone how Charlie had raped her and put a baby in her and how she'd gotten rid of it. She wanted to tell someone about how it had almost killed her. She knew God was punishing her for that. Happiness wasn't meant to be, not just yet, maybe not ever. She hadn't suffered enough. She didn't know if she would ever suffer enough over that. But then again, was Charlie suffering? He was the one who had brought this on. He was the one who had raped and impregnated her. Sure, she'd shot him in the foot but he hadn't suffered like her and that made her angry. It wasn't fair that he got off so easily when she had to carry the burden of guilt around and hate herself because she had little choice but to do what she had done.

"Ella," Frank said. "Sometimes things happen in life that has no rhyme or reason. It's not because you're a bad person, it's just because they happen. We all have troubles."

She'd had more than her fair share, though, and she felt it. She felt so bad for having the trouble, for being susceptible to such things. Maybe God was trying to tell her something.

"Ella?" he said softly.

She said, "Frank, I need to tell you something else."

"You can tell me anything."

She wanted to believe that but she couldn't. She stared at him, at his kind eyes and knew it was too much for him. He might want to kill Charlie Patterson for what he'd done to her. He was too good of a man not to take action on an issue like that. She'd revealed enough for one night. Maybe in time, she wouldn't even feel the need to tell him about Charlie. In fact, she'd like to forget about it herself.

She smiled and said, "I know that. I don't know how I know, but I know."

He smiled deeply at her, glad that they were finally beginning to communicate. "So tell me."

"It's just," she began but stopped. She stared at him and realized he could take care of her and that's what she wanted. She wanted to be taken care of the way she'd been by her parents when she was a little girl. She knew, also, that she could love this man. She could love him in a way she'd never loved anyone. It scared her, in a way, but it wasn't something she knew she could control. She remembered asking her father once, at the river, "What's love?" and had been surprised when he'd replied, "Everything." It didn't sound like him, her quiet father, but he'd said it and he had been right. Love was everything. It didn't make everything right, but it did make everything better.

"Ella?" he said.

"Nothing," she said. "I'm just being foolish."

He smiled at her. "Maybe we're both being foolish."

She laughed a little and shook her head at him, then became aware that they hadn't moved away from the door. And she became aware that she didn't want to. She didn't want to move one inch from Frank. She wanted him to touch her, to kiss her, to take the pain away, to make her forget about it. Didn't she deserve something nice like that? Maybe she had suffered enough. Maybe Frank was a gift from God for all the bad times.

"Do you want me to go now?" he asked.

"No," she said and shook her head. "I want you to..."

"What?"

She took a breath and stared up at him again. "I want to give you your goodnight kiss."

Frank grinned and bent down to her, to her lips. He brushed his against hers, sending shivers up and down her spine. She relaxed and pressed up against him and wanted him to do more. And he gave her another kiss, this one deeper. He took his time with the kiss, as any good lover would. Ella responded and began to kiss him back, taking his head in her hands and holding him still. She didn't want to let him get away. She wanted what he was offering. She needed it to heal her soul.

He pulled back and said, "We can stop now."

Ella shook her head and went in for another kiss and got what she wanted. She got it so much that she began to feel weak, then strong, then she began to want him. She wanted him in part because he made her forget everything as he kissed her. She'd never felt so alive as she did then.

Frank bent down and picked her up off the floor and carried her into the bedroom. They kept kissing as he carried her, then he placed her gently on the bed.

He pulled back and said again, "We can stop now."

Ella shook her head and held her arms out to, inviting him to her. She knew she was rushing it and she knew she should be a good girl and push him away but she didn't want to. She wanted him, it was that simple. It was a little sudden but she was tired, so tired of waiting for the "right" moment or the "right" man. She just wanted to feel, to feel wanted. That's all. And in that moment, Frank made her feel they way she always wanted to. And that was right. It was right by her.

"Are you sure?" he asked.

"I'm sure, Frank," she said. "I've never been more sure of anything in my life."

He bent down to her and gave her everything she'd needed for so long. They made love then and after he slept in her bed, holding her tightly throughout the night. When Ella woke in the morning, she looked over at him and smiled.

His eyes blinked open and he smiled back. "What is it?"

"Miss Sinclair would die if she saw you here right now," she said. "We're not supposed to have gentleman callers after ten."

"Gentlemen callers?" he asked with a raised eyebrow.

"Yeah, you know, gentleman callers," she said and studied him. He had a very bemused look on his face and was trying not to laugh. She didn't get it, then she did. For some reason, the term sounded absolutely ridiculous, like something an old lady would say, something *Miss Sinclair* would say. Before she could stop, she cracked up laughing.

Frank threw his head back and laughed with her. She laughed loudly, feeling the joy sweep through her body. That's when she knew for sure that Frank was her gift, her gift from God for everything bad that she had been through. And she was going to enjoy him.

People Talk

Ella had never been happier in that short year that followed. She was in love and a girl in love loves everything and everybody. She loved the sound of the crickets at night and the cool, sweet taste of ice cream. She loved the smell of burning wood in the fireplace and the way Frank met her every evening with a flower in his hand, even if it was raining and the flower got soggy. She loved the way she missed him as soon as they said goodnight and she loved the way he loved her, with total and utter abandonment, the way a man should always love a woman. The world was becoming lighter and more beautiful than it had ever been for Ella. She had never felt this way for anyone and it felt good to feel like that. The old Ella came out and she skipped to work, hummed as she did her chores around the apartment and smiled at strangers. She waited anxiously for

Frank every day to pick her up so they could go to his house and she could spend the night wrapped in his arms.

"We're going to have to stop doing this," she said one day. "People talk, Frank."

"And they always will, hopefully," he said.

She laughed at his joke and said, "We have to stop doing this."

"Doing what?" he asked and propped himself up on his elbow to stare at her. "Have I ever told you how absolutely beautiful you are, Ella?"

"God!" she squealed, shaking her fists. "You are so good with stuff like that!"

He laughed and nodded. "I took a class."

She grabbed his face and pulled his lips to hers and kissed him. He kissed her in return and pulled her under him, settling his bigger body on top of her smaller one. She kissed his neck until he pulled back.

"What is it?" she asked.

"Why did you say we were going to have to stop doing this?"

"People talk, Frank," she said.

"What are they saying, Ella?"

"They're saying," she whispered in his ear. "That we're laying up together."

"Huh," he said and considered that. "Does that mean we're going to hell?"

"God, I hope not," she replied. "Do you think we're going to hell?"

He laughed and said, "I don't guess we can do anything about it now, can we? I mean, we've already done all that bad stuff."

"Frank!" she squealed and slapped his arm. "Don't talk like that."

"Why not?"

"It's vulgar."

"'Vulgar'?" he said with a raised eyebrow. When she nodded, he said, "But anyways, yeah, people do talk and I reckon we might have to do something to shut 'em up."

"What do you mean?" she said in a panic. She didn't want to stop this. If it stopped, she'd die of heartbreak. Being away from Frank in the day made her feel this pain, this ache. It was a wonderful pain to feel, but a pain nonetheless. If he took that away from her, she couldn't imagine what she'd do.

"I mean," he said and reached across the bed to the nightstand. "We should do something about it."

Ella watched him, staring at the thick wooden nightstand then around the room, which was decorated with masculine, heavy wooden furniture. It was so comfortable in here, she never wanted to leave. When Frank pulled out a ring box, she knew she'd never have to.

"Please be my wife," he said and held out the box to her. "Will you marry me Miss Ella Muroc?"

"Yes!" she squealed and hugged his neck so hard, she nearly knocked him over.

He laughed and steadied her, then sat up. "You might want to check the ring out first, Ella, before you make your commitment."

"I don't care if you got it in a bubblegum machine," she said. "I love you, Frank, I love you so much!"

He grinned. "I love you too."

"So you want to marry me?" she asked.

"I do," he said and kissed the tip of her nose. "I want to do it right now, today."

She nodded, but then said, "No, we can't. I want my folks and brothers and sisters to be with me with I get married."

"That makes sense," he said.

"Can we have a nice wedding?" she asked. "I want a pretty white dress and a reception and all that."

"Sure," he said.

"We can?"

"We can," he said and nodded.

She stared at him and said, "How are you so good? How could you be this good to me?"

"Love makes fools out of the best of men," he said.

"You old meanie," she said and shook her head. "You old, sweet meanie."

"I'm not mean but I am a fool for you," he told her. "Don't ever forget that."

"I won't," she said. "And I plan on using it to my advantage."

"You already do," he said and grinned at her. "So when do you want to get married?"

The date popped into her head. "August twelfth."

"That's nearly six months away," he said.

"I know," she said. "But the thing is I want to plan the wedding and I want to go up and see my folks and tell them and then I want to—"

"I get the point," he said. "But if we ran down to the courthouse, you could move in here tomorrow."

She considered and said, "I just want it to be real from the get-go."

"It is real, Ella."

"I know," she said. "But I want to do it up right. You know, this might be my only wedding."

He laughed. "It better be."

She jumped off the bed. "I want to celebrate! I want a steak and a drink and a chocolate cake and then I want to come home and… Yeah."

He laughed, got up out of bed and went to her. "We can do that first."

"Well, if you insist, Mr. Jones."

"I insist," he said, then added. "Mrs. Jones."

That night, Frank took Ella to her favorite restaurant. As they dined, she talked about the wedding and how proud her parents were going to be of her. She was finally doing something right, something they could be proud of. She was going to make it up to them, she was going to set things right. She thought of little Olivia for a moment and her heart twisted in pain. One day, she'd go back to New York and she'd talk to Olivia. She'd make her understand she didn't give her up because she didn't love her, but because it was out of her hands. And it had been.

Frank said, "I think I need to meet your parents, Ella."

She nodded. "You will. I'm going to ask them to come here for the wedding, you know? They can stay at the house and we can... Well, we're going on a honeymoon, aren't we?"

"Of course," he said. "Where do you want to go?"

New York, she thought. But then she shook her head and said, "Somewhere tropical. Can we go to the beach? I've never seen the ocean, not really."

He smiled gently at her. Frank, himself, had traveled extensively, mostly for business. He'd gone into the world to see what it had to offer. He wanted Ella to travel, too. He wanted to give her the world.

Ella smiled back, then stared down at the beautiful engagement ring with its big diamond. She felt odd wearing something that cost so much money. She'd be sure to make sure nothing happened to it.

"Ella?" Frank said.

"What?" she asked and looked over at him.

He leaned across the table and whispered in her ear, "I want you. Right now."

She bit her lip. She wanted him too, right now.

"Let's go," he said and put a few bills on the table, then stood.

She followed him, slipping her hand into his. He led her out of the restaurant and gave the valet his ticket. They stood and waited. But Frank couldn't take it, he couldn't wait. He looked around and spotted the alley. He wanted her there.

"We'll be right back," he told one of the attendants. "We want to take a walk."

The attendant nodded and said, "We'll hold your car for you, Mr. Jones."

Frank nodded at him and he and Ella walked up the street a little, then he pulled her into the alley and pushed her up against the wall. She went with him, not saying a word. He sometimes did this. He would just stare at her and without muttering a syllable, push her back against the wall and kiss her. It was exciting when he took control like that and she couldn't get enough of it.

"Oh Frank," she moaned as he began to kiss her, touch her, take her. "I love you so much."

"I love you, too," he moaned and kissed her hard. He kissed her, thinking they were alone. And they were alone; they were alone in their own world. Nothing mattered to them but each other. Lovers are selfish in their quest to have one another and Frank and Ella were no different. It was all about them and their desire.

But they weren't necessarily alone. They were in a public place doing things lovers usually reserved for one another behind closed doors. They didn't care, though, mainly because they didn't think anyone else cared. And they didn't realize they were being watched. It was just a kiss they were sharing, albeit a passionate, lusty one. They'd shared kisses before and this one was no different.

Charlie Patterson had just come for dinner and a drink with a girl from the office. When he'd spotted Ella and Frank across the restaurant, he felt sick. He had heard rumors about their romance and it made him hate Frank Jones with a passion. He'd even gone as far as to cancel the insurance policies the company had purchased from him.

His father had chastised him for doing something "so stupid" because they had gotten the policies at a "steal."

And now Charlie was watching them. He'd abandoned his date to follow them out of the restaurant and had found them in the alley kissing. Charlie felt sick and had an impulse to tear them apart, to yell at Ella for breaking his heart. He was angry at her for giving Frank her love when she refused to give it to him.

As he watched them kiss, the way they were kissing so intimately, he felt a rage so strong he wanted to pound his fists on his chest. Ella moaned as they kissed, wanting more. Charlie knew then that they'd been intimate before, just by the way she was responding to Frank, in a way she'd never responded to him. The way she had refused to respond to him. He felt sick and he wanted to hurt Frank Jones, but then he wanted to hurt Ella more.

He couldn't take it anymore. He turned away and went back into the restaurant and grabbed his date's hand. He dragged her out and into the car and then he took her home. When they got inside, he kissed her hard and she allowed it. She liked Charlie and wanted to be intimate with him, mainly because she wanted to marry a man like him. She didn't know his heart was with someone else but wouldn't have cared. Things like that didn't matter, so she allowed Charlie to do whatever he wanted. But all he wanted was for her to be Ella.

After it was over, he got out of bed and said, without looking at her, "Leave."

She felt a flush of embarrassment and hissed, "You bastard."

He ignored her and walked out of the room.

High Time

Charlie Patterson did try to move on. He did try to forget about Ella but the image of her and Frank Jones making out in that alley was burned into his brain. Why couldn't it be him? Why couldn't she love him like she loved that son of a bitch? He was so much better than Frank Jones, so much more educated. He had more money, more everything.

But he didn't have Ella.

He knew he was obsessed and occasionally he would feel shame for his feelings about her. But he couldn't get his head around the fact that she just didn't want him, that she never had. To his credit, he did try to forget about her. He went on a lot of dates with different women and he searched for what he'd found in Ella. But he always came up short.

Then it happened. It was inevitable and the day Charlie learned of Ella's plans to marry Frank Jones, something changed in him. Of course, everyone at the office was invited to her wedding. Everyone, that was, except Charlie Patterson.

In a matter of months, she told everyone, she would be gone, so they'd better start appreciating her. She laughed as she said it and everyone around her laughed too. No one knew how right she was.

It was in early May that Charlie realized that he had to make Ella change her mind. He couldn't let her marry Frank Jones. He knew he was the better man. He would have to make her understand it.

He began to follow her, trying to get up enough nerve to approach and beg her not to marry Frank. But he never could find it and, in the early morning fog when he saw her leave her apartment with two suitcases, he knew he was about to lose her forever. He felt a panic so strong that he did what he selfishly thought any man in love would do. He decided to take the matter into his own hands.

He followed her to the train station and watched her from afar. He knew she was leaving. He knew she was moving on. She was going to be gone soon. He had to stop her. The clock was ticking. He had to tell her how he felt or it would be too late. She needed to know how sorry he was about all that had happened. He needed her forgiveness, then he could move on. Most of all, he had to tell her how much he loved her, even if that love was making a fool out of him. Even if it was making him crazy, she needed to know.

And it was high time she did. Charlie took that step towards Ella that he would regret for the rest of his life.

Ella went to the train station early that morning, looking forward to seeing her family. Life was so good for her that she couldn't help but walk around with a smile. After she checked her two suitcases, she went to the train and was about to board when she remembered she hadn't bought the tobacco her father liked. She always liked to get everyone a gift of some kind. She walked back to the small newsstand but then noticed it was closed because it was so early.

"Ella?"

She turned to see Charlie Patterson approaching her. While she was annoyed, she wasn't surprised. She had seen him hanging around places where she was for the last few months. She didn't realize what he was doing, mostly because she thought if she ignored him and didn't engage him in conversation, he would leave her alone. Obviously, that tactic wouldn't work with someone like Charlie. She groaned and said, "What are you doing here?"

"Where are you going?"

"Home," she said. "Why are you here?"

"Ella," he said and took her arm. "We need to talk."

"You need to leave me alone," she said and jerked her arm away. "I thought we'd already talked about this. Didn't you get the point?"

"No, I didn't," he said and took her arm again.

"I have to go," she hissed. "Let me go. I have to catch that train."

"You can catch the next one," he said and steered her away from the newsstand.

"No!" she hissed.

"Yeah," he said. "I think you should."

Charlie walked her away from the newsstand even though she swatted and swore at him. There weren't many people there because it was so early. Then he took a handkerchief out of his pocket and pressed it over her mouth and nose, making her breathe the ether that would put her out.

"What are you doing?" she hissed and shook her head.

"Shh," he said. "Just come with me."

"Let...let me..." she murmured, her eyes heavy. "What'd you do?"

He didn't answer and kept walking her. She was about to pass out and couldn't keep her feet moving. They were almost to the door. A few more steps and his car was parked on the curb. Charlie bent to pick her up when an old man approached them.

"That girl alright?" the old man asked.

Charlie nodded. "It's my wife. She's passed out again."

"Oh?"

"Having a hard time with the baby," he said and patted her stomach.

"Huh," he said. "Need any help?"

"No, thank you," Charlie said and picked her up, then stared at the man who was still standing there looking at him. "What are you doing? Do you need help?"

"I don't know," the old man said. "I don't even know how I got here."

Charlie stared at him and realized the old man was senile. He felt bad for the man and smiled at him. The old man smiled back and muttered, "I think my wife might be waiting for me."

And then he hurried away.

Ella had never been in Charlie Patterson's house, but when she came to, she wasn't that impressed. She wasn't impressed with anything about Charlie Patterson, even his large home with paneled walls and a big stone fireplace. Fancy artwork hung on the walls and plush couches sat on a shiny wooden floor which was covered here and there with Chinese rugs.

"Are you awake?"

Ella looked up to see Charlie standing in front of her. She was lying on one of the couches. Her head throbbed. What had he done to her?

He bent down in front of her and said, "I was wondering when you were going to wake up."

She sat up. Her head spun for a minute and she had to lie back down for a second. Charlie pushed a glass of water into her hands and she eyed him before drinking a sip, then threw the remainder into his face.

He shook his head and wiped his face off with the back of his arm. Then he took the glass and sat it on the table. Ella watched him, then was horrified when he sat next to her and took her hand and kissed it.

"I love you, Ella," he said. "That's all I wanted to tell you. I love you."

Ella was not a cruel-hearted person and her heart went out to Charlie at that moment. She didn't want him hurting over her. In fact, she hated the idea of his liking her so much that he would do something like this. It made her skin crawl, sure, but at the same time, it made her heart ache.

She stared at him sadly and said, "Charlie, it's not love if the other person doesn't love you back."

"Then what is it?"

"I don't know but it's not love," she said. She'd read a novel where the main character had been obsessed like Charlie was with her. The man did all kinds of crazy things before he finally gave up. But Charlie wasn't about to give up. He would break her. She knew that was his plan.

"No, it's love," he said.

Ella sighed and looked around. "Charlie, what do you want with me? I'm just a poor girl, nothing special."

"But you are special," he said and scooted closer to her. "You're so special to me."

"But you think I'm beneath you," she said. "And when I turned you down, you couldn't stand that someone like me did that to you. That's why you're acting like this, Charlie."

"No," he said. "I've never thought for one minute that you were beneath me. I just said that to hurt your feelings."

"If only that were true."

He couldn't win with her. Why did he even try? Why did he do this to himself? To her? He was playing a dangerous game but he couldn't stop himself.

"Let me go, Charlie," she said, trying to reason with him. "Let me go and I won't tell a soul, I promise you. I promise you I won't tell anyone. We'll forget about it, I swear."

"Break up with Frank Jones and marry me instead."

That flew all over her. *How dare he?* How dare he kidnap her and then have the nerve to ask her to break up with the one man who was willing to stick by her? How dare he do all this to her? All of a sudden, she was livid and she was screaming, "Are you crazy?! God! What is wrong with you?"

He grabbed her arm and said, "If you'd just listen to me, Ella—"

She swatted at him. "Let me go! My daddy's waiting on me at the train station! If he finds out what you've done to me, he'll put a bullet in you, Charlie!"

He didn't let her go.

She calmed down a little, then swatted at him again. "Stop it!"

He tried to push her back on the couch. Though she was still a little groggy, she jumped up and started off. He grabbed at her but she sidestepped him and ran off. He caught her at the door and pushed her back against it. Then he released her. She glowered at him, hating him so much that it scared her; but the hate felt right, something she felt she needed to feel.

"Damn you, Charlie," she screamed, her fists shaking. "Damn you to hell, Charlie Patterson! I hate you so much! I just hate you! God forgive me for how much I hate you!"

Charlie dropped his head but he wasn't about to give up. He was going to break her. He was going to break her down and then she'd love him like he loved her.

"Well, I guess you got me," she hissed. "You got me Charlie. You finally got me. Are you happy now? Does it make you happy to make someone else so miserable? What is it about you that wants me to suffer, Charlie? Why? Why won't you just leave me alone?"

For the first time, Charlie realized how much she really hated him. She hated him so much, hated what he was doing to her, what he had done and what he would do. For an instant, he hated himself, then reverted back to wanting to control her. There was no reasoning with her. She was out of control. He knew he had to make her understand but she was doing something to him, the same sort of thing she'd done that night he'd hurt her. He couldn't put his finger on it, on what she was doing, but it was pushing at something deep inside of him, making a rage come out so strong it almost scared him. That's when Charlie snapped. He grabbed her. But he had to stop, he had to stop himself. He couldn't stop himself. *Stop it, stop it, stop it!* He stopped and found that she was on the floor now, not moving. What had he done? Had he beaten her? His head swam and he held it, warding off the memory of him placing his hands on her, harming her, making her shut up. Why was he doing this? He was making Ella make up for everything. Ella... His eyes opened and he stared at her, there on the floor. What had he done? And why had he done it? And why couldn't he help himself?

He bent to her, pulled her into his arms and cradled her head. "Oh, God, Ella, I'm so sorry."

"Sure you are, Charlie," she mumbled. "Sure you are."

He tried to kiss her but she started laughing crazily. He pulled back and stared at her in horror.

"What are you gonna do, Charlie?" she asked, and chuckled like it was the funniest thing, then her face hardened and she spat the words, "Kiss me? Romance me? What are you gonna do? Are you gonna try again? Are you gonna put another baby in me?"

His mouth fell open and he stared at her in disbelief. "What are you talking about?"

She laughed more deeply and shook her head slightly. "You gonna try and put a baby in there? In me? Let me tell you something, you can't."

He moved away from her and stood. She stood with him and advanced on him.

"No, you're not and you're not because I can't have babies no more. I can't have any, thanks to you, Charlie. Thanks to you!"

She was screaming now with rage and she was beating her small fists on his chest and face. He warded her off but she didn't let up.

"You took that away from me!" she screamed. "Damn you to hell! You took it away from me! You stole my life! You stole my babies!"

He finally threw her off. She landed on the floor and glared up at him. He asked before he could stop himself, "Did you have my baby?"

She laughed menacingly. "Are you kidding me? Are... you...kidding...me?!"

He looked away from her. Charlie suddenly knew what she had done and it infuriated him. Why hadn't she come to him? He would have helped her, married her the second she told him she was with child. But he knew why she hadn't come to him. He felt sick, so sick that he couldn't control himself. He hated himself for hurting her like that, for taking what innocence she had left and destroying it. He was no better than an animal and he knew it. Her lip was bleeding now. He had backhanded her so hard that her lip bled. God, he prayed, please stop me before I really hurt her.

"Cat got your tongue, Charlie?" she slurred, laughing, then wiped her lip. "You can do your worse but you'll never—never!—top that one."

She was right. She'd been stripped of everything that ever meant anything. And it angered her that this man had done these things and, not only that, but he continued to hurt her. He wouldn't let up. She suddenly wished she'd shot him in the heart that day in her apartment when she'd had the chance. She'd be in jail, sure, but at least she wouldn't be here. It was that kind of thinking that began to scare her, that began to make her wonder why he was driving her to this dark place, to this black anger. But she wanted him to hurt. She wanted him to feel a little something.

She said, "Charlie no matter what you do to me, it couldn't make me feel any worse. Nothing—you can't do nothing to me!"

Charlie hated himself. He hated his obsession for Ella. He hated his consuming love for her. He hated longing for a woman who did not want him. He wanted to move on, but couldn't. He'd done his best but life wouldn't give him what he wanted. What was stopping him from moving on? Her, she was stopping him. She was too good, too much. She was all he ever wanted, all he thought about. It was unrequited love, sure, but it was so much more than that. It was a deep soul connection they had and neither could deny that, for some reason, fate had brought them together. If she would just stop struggling with it, stop fighting it, everything would be okay.

"I'm sorry," Charlie said and meant it.

She spat in his face. "That's what I think of your 'sorry'."

He nodded and wiped his face off with the back of his hand. "Why don't you love me?"

She was stunned for a moment. But then she was livid again. "Love you? How could I love you? You don't love someone who traps you like a wild animal. You don't love someone who treats you like dirt. You don't love someone who imprisons you. But most of all, you don't love someone like you, Charlie."

"Why not?"

"You're not worthy of my love, that's why," she said. "Or the love of any decent woman. Hell, you'd be lucky to even get a street whore to like you."

She was right. That's what he couldn't stand. What she was saying was what Charlie felt about himself, deep down, but covered up and ran from anytime it tried to rear its ugly little head. He stared at her and he hurt, he hurt so bad. He hurt knowing she didn't love him, that he had made her hate him. But then he knew what he was doing. He was acting out so she would reach out and give him that approval he always longed for but never got from anyone. He hurt her so she would forgive him. Inside of the forgiveness was the love, the real love he longed for. He didn't know love didn't work like that. But in his twisted mind, Ella was going to make up for everything. It was a large burden to put on someone else but Charlie had laid it on Ella's shoulders then got angry when she shrugged off her duty of being his everything.

"Just love me," he said. "Just love me, Ella."

"How could I?" she asked, almost sadly, though she was tired from the beating. "How could I, Charlie?"

"How could you not?" he asked. "I'm a good man."

"Yeah," she said sarcastically. "They sure don't make 'em like you, Charlie."

That made his blood boil. He couldn't help it if he'd found someone he wanted to love. Why couldn't she see how much better she made his life? That love, that love she had and gave away to everyone except him made him feel worthless. Why, for once, wasn't he picked? Why wasn't he the one someone wanted with abandon? He was a good man, deep in his soul, there was good in Charlie Patterson. He just couldn't make anyone see it for the life of him.

He glared at her. "Sometimes you make me so mad I could just kill you."

She felt chills, but she didn't give into them. She stared at him and wondered how and why they'd gotten here. She could have cried from the thought of it, from the pain that seared her heart. We never retreat to love, we run from it. The only thing we react to is fear. She reacted by jumping up and running, trying to get to the door.

Charlie caught her around the waist and threw her down on the floor. She screamed so loudly it rattled his ears. He pulled back from her. She sat up and glared at him. She would hurt him if it killed her. She was going to make this man feel what she had felt, all that pain and misery. She attacked with the only real weapon a woman has against a man—her tongue.

"Let me tell you something about yourself, Charlie," Ella said, laughing a little. "You're the kind of man who hires a whore and after you're done with her, you beat her."

He backhanded her over the comment. She didn't care. Let him beat her, let him do his worst. She was done with him. All she had to do was get through this and after, she was would make sure Charlie got his. She would tell Frank everything and tell her daddy. She would tell the newspapers, she'd tell everyone about Charlie Patterson and the torment he'd put her through. Everyone needed to know what kind of person he really was.

"You know what?" she said suddenly, as if she'd perked up. "I'm not gonna tell my daddy what you did to me. I'm gonna do what he'd do. I'm going to kill you myself, Charlie."

He wasn't the least impressed with her threat. Mainly because she could barely move now. Besides that, he didn't think she had it in her. But he'd brought this out in her, this hate. Maybe it was self-preservation. It would be her or him, she knew instinctively. Why it had come to this, she didn't know, didn't care anymore. Her survival instinct clicked on inside of her and that made her not care what happened to him anymore. He'd pushed her down so far in the dirt that she was covered with filth. She'd adopted his rage and made it her own. It wasn't becoming of her, but it fit right.

"Shut up, Ella," he said. "Stop talking like that."

"Rot in hell, Charlie," she said. "Rot in hell."

"You first," he said.

Again, Ella felt chills. Her fight or flight instinct kicked in and she told herself to get the hell out of there—anyway she could. The adrenaline gave her a surge of power.

She jumped up and, for some reason, ran up the stairs. He was hot on her heels. She screamed and ran down the hall, trying to get into one of the rooms, but the doors were heavy and wouldn't give. She looked over at her shoulder to see him approaching and screamed, "Please, Charlie, you don't know want you're doing! It's time you stopped! Stop it, Charlie!"

He grabbed her and tried to kiss her again. She clawed at his face, leaving scratches. He hollered out and held his bleeding face. She got away and headed to the stairs again, determined to get down them and out the door.

He limped/ran after her and yelled, "Just give me a minute, Ella! One minute! One minute!"

She was at the top of the stairs when he yelled that. She turned and stared at him. He was coming at her again. She had to get down the stairs. She started to run but then her heel caught on the carpet and she slipped and fell, tumbling over and over until she got to the bottom of the stairs, where she landed on her head. Just like her big brother, Edward, it was a fall that would do her in.

"*ELLA*!" Charlie screamed and ran down to her. "Oh, my God, Ella!"

He stopped at her body and walked around her, staring at her, not believing for a minute she was dead. He bent down next to her and shook her, yelling, "You wake up now! Ella! Wake up!"

She didn't.

"Wake up now, Ella," he said softly.

She didn't respond. He stared at her and knew that she was gone. But he didn't accept it as true. His mind comprehended but his heart refused to believe. He put her head in his lap and sat there for a long time and told her all the things she'd refused to listen to. He told her that it could have been so beautiful, that when a man loves a woman like he loved her, it was hard to stay in control. He told her he was sorry and that if she'd just wake up, he'd make it all up to her.

"It was an accident," he said. "Just a little accident. Nothing special. We'll get through it, Ella, we'll get through it."

He knew they wouldn't get through it. A sob caught in his throat and he almost doubled over with grief. But it had been an accident, unintentional. He hadn't meant to hurt her. But if he hadn't intended to do it, why had he brought her here?

He couldn't think about that right now. No, he wasn't going to think about all that stuff. She was here with him now and that's all he'd ever wanted.

"Would you like a new car?" he asked her and pushed the hair out of her face. "I want to buy you a Cadillac. Or would you like a Lincoln? You want a Lincoln like mine, honey? I'll get you one."

He stopped talking and wiped the tears off his face. He nodded and rocked her, as if he were rocking her to sleep. "When you wake up, we're going to talk and then you can leave. When you wake up, it's all going to be better for us, Ella. We're going to live a good, good life. You won't regret it for a minute, either, once you see how good I can be to you. I love you."

She didn't respond.

"Yeah, you keep sleeping," he said. "You need your rest. When you wake up, we'll eat something. Are you hungry? You will be when you wake up."

But Ella would never wake up again.

Like An Angel

A month following Ella's disappearance, Jean Stephens was asked to clean out Ella's desk. It was apparent that she wasn't coming back to work. As she did it, tears spilled from her eyes.

As she worked, she heard some chatter and looked up to see Charlie Patterson talking to an executive of some kind. He was speaking politely and even once seemed to make a joke. He was always doing that, always joking, trying to get everyone to like him. How could he do that after what he'd done? How could he? How could he stand there and crack a joke and not care? He should pay, shouldn't he? Everyone should know what he had done, what he was capable of. Jean, herself, wasn't sure what Charlie had done, but she knew he had *something* to do with Ella's disappearance. And there he was joking—laughing!—like nothing had happened. Something in Jean snapped and before she knew it, she was running up to him.

"You did it, didn't you?" she hissed as she came at him.

Charlie jumped away and stared at Jean. He'd briefly had his eye on her just before he'd turned it towards Ella. But after Ella, he hadn't given her a second glance.

She ran at him and beat his chest with her fists, "You did it! I know you did it!"

Two men standing nearby pulled her off Charlie, who stood there frozen. As they dragged her away, she kept screaming, "You did it! I know you did it! Admit it, Charlie! Admit it!"

"What is she talking about?" the executive asked Charlie.

"I have no idea," he said.

Charlie's father told him to take some time off after that. He understood that the employees needed to get over Ella's disappearance. She was a favorite, after all and when things like that happened, people needed time to heal. Charlie wanted to tell him what he had done but he knew his old man would never understand. He wanted to tell someone, but he couldn't bring himself to confess.

Charlie's father also fired Jean Stephens. She was now out of work and out of hope. In addition to that, she got a visit from a couple of guys Mr. Patterson sent over to her apartment. They told her to keep her mouth shut, they didn't say about what, but then again, they didn't have to.

Jean really began to hate Charlie Patterson with a vengeance after that.

But she knew there would be retribution for Charlie Patterson. She was waiting for that day. When that day came, God would tell her what to do and He'd point her in the right direction.

It would take almost a year for justice to be served. Meanwhile, Jean waited patiently. She got another job and got married. During all this, she prayed every night and she knew in time that God would come through.

When she saw Doc Muroc standing in front of her old apartment house, she knew the day had come. She was so happy to see him standing there she almost skipped to his side and took his hand. But she played it cool, played it like she was just passing by. She didn't tell him she passed by on a regular basis or that Miss Sinclair had told her that he sometimes visited. She didn't tell him that she knew he would do the right thing or that she knew she had to talk to him about Charlie. She didn't tell him these things because there was no need to. As she walked up to him, she thought of how he stood there, so stoically, so ready to do what had to be done. He was like an angel standing there, ready to take care of things.

So ye ask, so shall ye receive…

Doc watched Charlie Patterson. The man walked with a limp, that's how he knew he was the right man. He was the man who had been in front of Ella's apartment that day. He was the man in the window. After all this time, Doc had finally found him.

Doc watched him and wondered why. He was a good looking man in nice clothes. He drove a nice car and seemed to be well-off. Doc even saw him bring a girl back to his house later that night. She left after about an hour. This man lived well, seemed nice enough and didn't look like he'd hurt a fly. But Doc knew outward appearances rarely indicate what's going on inside.

It didn't take Doc long to make his plans. He didn't like putting things off, either. It was time to get the job done. So, on the second day, around six in the afternoon, Doc made his move and walked up to Charlie's front door and knocked on it.

When Charlie opened the door, he immediately knew who the old man was. He knew because Ella had had a family portrait on her desk. Charlie had asked about it once before they went on their first date and she had told him who everyone was—her mother, her brothers and sisters. Then she paused at her father and laughed a little. "Those old overalls! Can you believe Mommy couldn't get him to wear a suit? And he's got one, a good one she bought in Middlesboro. But he loves his overalls. I told Mommy that we'll probably have to bury him in them."

Her comments had struck Charlie as funny and he recalled the story of her father many times after that, imagining him in those overalls. He also felt a little jealousy that he didn't feel the same way about his old man that Ella felt for hers.

So, Charlie knew who Doc was and he knew what he wanted. He knew that he was searching for his daughter. He didn't have to be told. He had known this day would come and it had seemed to take a long time. He had dreaded it but now, as Doc stood in front of him, he was somehow relieved.

"You Charlie Patterson?" Doc asked.

Charlie nodded and stared at the old man, wondering how a beautiful creature like Ella could have come from someone like him. His wrinkled and worn face looked almost like leather from too many nights in the mines. His old boots made Charlie's heart go out to him a little. He stood awkwardly, too, sort of leaning forward and bending at the knees because of the pain he suffered as a result of sitting on them in the mines. Doc never complained of the pain but he did eye a chair in Charlie's foyer for a moment before pulling a picture of Ella out of his jacket.

Doc thrust the picture at Charlie. "That's my girl and I reckon you know something about her."

Charlie swallowed hard and shook off the picture.

Doc thrust it at him again. "Take a look at her. I bet you'd remember her if you ever saw her."

"I don't know what you're talking about."

"Boy, don't think you can fool this old man," he said. "Take a look at my girl."

Charlie reluctantly took the picture and stared at Ella. A lump rose in his throat when he saw her smiling face. He pushed the picture back at Doc. "Would you like to come in?"

"She in there?" he asked.

"No," Charlie snapped. "Why do you say that?"

"I'll come in," Doc said, ignoring his question. He walked into the spacious foyer, which was almost as big as his whole house, and looked around. He wasn't impressed with it. Nothing about this man would ever impress him. Doc usually gave a man the benefit of the doubt but with this one, he didn't. He knew this man had done something and it would only be a matter of time before he confirmed his suspicions. He could feel it.

"This way," Charlie said and led him into the living room.

Doc followed him, then declined his offer for coffee. "I just come to find out what you know about my daughter."

Charlie nodded and sat down, lighting a cigarette. "All I know about her is that she was a secretary at my business. She seemed nice enough, but we never had occasion to talk."

Doc raised his eyebrows at Charlie's educated way of speaking. He didn't let his fine manners or polite talk fool him. He didn't know much, but he knew people and he could see through just about anyone. He knew Charlie was side-stepping him but Doc wasn't so easily fooled.

Charlie could tell that he was doing a poor job of lying and for a moment, wanted to confess, to get it out in the open. But he knew with confession came responsibility and he didn't want to go to prison, even if it had, technically, been an accident.

"She was gettin' married," Doc said and took off his hat, then ran his hand through his hair. "You know that fella Frank Jones?"

Charlie nodded slightly.

"What do you think of him?" he asked.

"Supposedly, he's very volatile," Charlie said and puffed on his cigarette. "I heard some rumors at work that he had an unhealthy obsession for Ella."

Doc knew he wasn't telling the truth. The man was a liar and if there's one thing Doc couldn't stand was a liar. Frank Jones was twice the man this one was. And Doc liked Frank Jones, and when Doc liked someone, they were golden in his eyes and he wouldn't stand for anyone to talk about them.

"That's all I know," Charlie said, stubbing out his cigarette in an ashtray then standing. "If you'll excuse me, I have somewhere to be."

"No," Doc said, not moving. "Your place is with me right now."

Charlie stared at him. "What do you mean?"

"Boy, I'm going to level with you," Doc said, leaning forward. "I've been looking for my girl for over a year. A year ago she was supposed to come home but she didn't show up. We got her suitcases and lot of grief. Her mommy's been killing herself with it. My other kids are sick with it. Now, between you and me, I know you know something. The sooner you give it up, the sooner we can both get on with it."

Charlie nodded.

Doc stood and said, "I come here for my girl and I ain't leaving without her."

Charlie understood that no matter what he said to Doc, how much he lied, the old man would not let up until he confessed. But Charlie also thought about what a relief it would be to confess. But then he thought about the responsibility of doing something like that. He considered for a moment before coming up with the perfect solution. Then Charlie did what he did best, he lied, "I'll take you to her. I think I know where she might be."

"I figured you might," Doc said and felt a surge of panic. *This was it.* He knew this was it. His skin began to tingle and his face grew red-hot as his heart beat rapidly inside his chest. *This was it.* It was all coming to an end. The end had always seemed so far away and now that he was faced with this closure, he almost wanted to turn and run.

But he hadn't traveled so far to run from the truth and the truth was what he'd always been seeking. Without a word, they got into Charlie's Lincoln and drove. They drove about thirty miles out of town, coming to a dirt road, which Charlie pulled on to. He drove a few more miles and then parked the car.

"She's in the quarry over there."

That meant...that meant... That meant... Doc forced himself to stop feeling the barrage of emotions that were coming at him at that moment. This was no time for them, so he concentrated on his task of finding Ella. He asked, "You put her in there?"

"Yeah," Charlie said.

"Let's go have a look-see," Doc said and got out of the car.

Charlie followed him to the edge of the quarry and stared at Doc, trying to read his face. He couldn't know what he was feeling or thinking. He suddenly felt so bad for what he'd done and he wanted Doc to know the truth.

"Why don't you go ahead and tell me what happened, boy?" Doc said.

"I didn't mean to do it," Charlie said. "It was an accident."

Doc stared at him. "How's that?"

"She fell down the stairs at my house."

"She fell?"

"And hit her head," Charlie said and looked away from him quickly.

"She's...uh..." Doc stopped and prayed that he wouldn't confirm his suspicions, prayed that this was all a sick joke of some kind, prayed that he wouldn't have to hear what was about to come out of Charlie's mouth.

"She's dead."

So she was dead. She was gone. Dear sweet, little Ella, his girl, his eldest, the cutest freckles that ran across her nose... That giggle, the giggle that had turned into such a nice laugh as she aged. The long, dark hair and those bright blue eyes. Ella, his pride and joy, was dead. Dead. Dead to him and to the rest of the world. Dead. Gone. Her mother would go crazy with the news. Ruth wouldn't ever be able to handle this. Doc was having a hard time himself.

Doc suddenly understood what death meant and that meant he would not be apologizing to her for the awful things he'd done. He would not ever welcome another grandbaby from her into his life. He would not attend her wedding nor would she be there for him when he got old and sick. There was like this break had happened once Doc let the truth sink in. It was a hard break and Doc felt like someone had punched him in the gut. His knees almost buckled from beneath him. He wanted to jump in the water himself. He didn't know if he could take what was coming at him, didn't know if he wanted to. He wasn't too surprised when Charlie started breaking down, crying and pleading with him, begging for his forgiveness. But he wasn't listening to him. All he could hear was that word, "dead." Ella was dead. His girl was gone. There was a roaring in his ears then, a loud sound like a cold wind. He thought for a moment that he would pass out, that he would die. He almost wanted to. If he was dead, he wouldn't have to deal with this. He'd only wanted to find her alive so he could tell her how sorry he was. He'd only wanted that one chance to have that one conversation to make things right. Now his chance was gone.

"I didn't mean to do it," Charlie cried. "I swear to God. She ran away from me and then she fell down the stairs and hit her head."

Doc stayed detached. He forced himself to detach. It was getting dark and night was coming. Charlie's blathering went on for a long time but Doc didn't absorb most of it. All he could think about was Ella, who was dead and the fact that this man had killed her. He didn't know what he would do now, now that he knew for sure what happened to her. What would he do now that he'd found the truth that had eluded him for so long? The man was pathetic, crying and slobbering over himself with the knowledge of what he'd done. He was suffering, that's what he was doing. Doc had suffered, too. A lot more than this man.

Doc looked up through the trees at the darkening sky and, when he spotted an old raccoon sitting at the top of one, he smiled. It was as if the old raccoon had been waiting on him all along, as if he'd been waiting for years to see Doc. And Doc was sure glad to see him, too. It was then that nothing seemed to matter anymore. It was like a switch had been flipped and Doc came to clarity. It dawned on him that things with Charlie and this trip here wasn't exactly right. Doc knew that if he didn't get a hold of himself and his emotions then he wouldn't be leaving these woods. And he knew, somehow he knew, that Charlie was lying to him about Ella. Maybe it was wishful thinking. Maybe he was lying to himself. But Doc was no fool. So, with that knowledge, Doc focused on the raccoon in the tree. That raccoon was his warning. He knew it, the raccoon knew it and Charlie would soon know it, too.

"I'm gonna get you, boy," he said to the raccoon, nodding. "I've come for you."

Charlie stopped talking and stared at Doc in fright.

Doc pointed up and said, "If I just had my gun," he said, then stared at Charlie. "If I just had my gun."

Charlie's eyes grew wide at his comment and he looked up, too, to see the large raccoon. He looked back at Doc and wondered what, exactly, he meant.

"Boy," Doc said. "You ever been huntin'?"

"No," Charlie said. "Well, I have, but it's been years."

"Tonight would be a good night for huntin', wouldn't it?" Doc asked. "If we had us a good old coon dog right now, boy, we'd be set."

Charlie wondered if the old man was crazy.

"If I just had old Smokey Joe," Doc mumbled, remembering his best dog. That dog could tree any coon, anytime, anywhere. For a moment, in the midst of the memory of his favorite dog, Doc forgot why he was there, with Charlie, and just thought of the good times he'd had with his dog. It was a distant memory that was all but gone. All he had left was the remnants, scattered visions of himself and the dog and the dark woods late at night. He remembered Smokey Joe's barking, too, a loud, bloodhound-dog wail that pieced his ears.

Charlie cleared his throat, hoping to get Doc's attention back. Doc glanced at him, then looked back up at the raccoon, smiling at it. The raccoon ignored him and slept.

"Ah!" Doc said and slapped Charlie on the back. "Come on, boy, let's go huntin'. We'll build us a fire then we'll track us a coon."

Charlie stared after Doc who was walking away from him, deeper into the woods. It was getting dark and an ominous feeling came over Charlie. He should leave the old man there. But he couldn't. He had work to do and he had to finish up this one loose end.

He followed Doc into the woods and watched as he made a fire in the middle of a small clearing. The fact was, Charlie liked the old man. He just couldn't tell if the old man liked him or not. He hated what he had to do but it was a necessary evil.

Doc had camped plenty of times in the woods. He'd be out hunting with his dogs late at night and the time would pass quickly, so he'd build himself a fire or he'd help the other men build it. They would sit around the fire and listen for the dogs to howl, which would indicate they had treed a coon. As they waited, they'd talk. They would talk about life and about their families. The hunting was more social than any of them would dare to admit. Ruth had once commented, "You old men sit around and gossip like a bunch of old women. It ain't got much to do with the coon." He'd made no comment.

Doc made the fire and sat back on a log. His knees ached but a pinch of tobacco took his mind off the pain. He chewed silently and watched the fire, noticing that a big branch was sticking out, about six inches round. Doc kept his eye on the branch. He didn't want the dry grass to catch fire.

Doc hadn't said a word in a long time, only chewed his tobacco. Charlie hadn't spoken either. They both sat and watched the fire. Doc spat to the side, wiped his mouth off and then turned to Charlie. "So you killed my girl, did you?"

Charlie shook his head. "It really was an accident."

"I don't reckon I believe in accidents," Doc said. "What was she doing at your house that day?"

"She had spent the night."

"Oh, no," Doc said. "Don't go lying on her like that. What was doing at your house?"

"I brought her there," he said and stared at his shoes.

"Get her from the train station?"

Charlie nodded. "I did."

"So what was you intending on doing with her once you got her home?"

"Nothing," he muttered and stared back at Doc. "I just wanted to talk to her."

"About what?"

Charlie's face became animated and he wanted Doc to know how much he'd loved Ella. "I loved her and I wanted her to know that. I really loved her but she… I just loved her so much. I really did."

"Lots of boys loved Ella, though," he said. "You the only one who killed her."

"I didn't kill her," Charlie said. "She fell down the stairs."

"Sure you didn't push her?" he asked and spat out the remainder of his tobacco.

"No," Charlie muttered. "I didn't push her."

Doc nodded but didn't respond. He wiped his mouth off with a handkerchief he'd pulled from his pocket and sighed. He had been right. It was turning out to be a long night.

Charlie stood up and began to pace crazily. "She was driving me crazy. She was always on my mind, in it… Oh, God. It just got out of control. I wasn't myself. I just wasn't myself."

Doc eyed him but still didn't respond. He hadn't made his mind up what to do. The man was probably telling the truth, that she'd slipped on the stairs, but of course, she wouldn't have slipped if he hadn't brought her there. Why had he done such a crazy thing? None of that really mattered though. She was still dead and this man was responsible.

Charlie started talking then, almost fanatically, insanely, "She just wouldn't stop. I tried to make her be quiet but she kept screaming, calling me names, telling me things about myself that I never wanted to believe. I didn't mean to hit her, not like that. But she wouldn't stop talking, mouthing. I don't know how it happened. I really don't know, but she was so…so little and I hit her. I didn't mean to, I really didn't. I was so ashamed that I had but then she got up and ran up the stairs and I told myself to stop, to leave, to do anything but I ran after her."

Doc stared into the fire and imagined what this man had done to his daughter, how he'd beaten her. He told the anger he felt to settle down, that he'd contend with it later. Right now, he had to concentrate on Charlie.

"God, I'm such a bastard," he said and held his head. "I'm so sorry for what I did. I didn't mean to do it but there was something that took over me. I don't know what it was but I couldn't help myself. I hate what I did, Doc, I hate what I did to her. I hate myself."

Doc eyed him for a moment before returning his gaze to the fire.

"I chased her," Charlie said more calmly, as if her were recounting a story he'd told a million times. "I told her to just calm down. I think I did anyway. I just wanted her to love me and she told me she couldn't ever love someone like me. And then it was just crazy. It happened so quickly. She was there, at the top of the stairs, and then she was… She fell down the stairs and I heard her scream as she fell. I was frozen as I watched because I knew I couldn't do anything to stop what was going to happen and I knew it was happening because I started it. And then everything stopped, it got quiet. I knew she was gone, and she was. She was gone."

Doc blanched. He could imagine his pretty daughter doing just that and it was the image that had haunted him for so long, the image of her dying.

Charlie went on, "I didn't know what to do. I wanted to bring her back so bad but I couldn't. I sat there with her all afternoon but then I realized she wasn't coming back no matter how bad I wanted it or how hard I prayed."

Doc squeezed his eyes shut.

"I didn't have any other choice," Charlie said. "I put her in my car and I brought her to that quarry over there and threw her in. That's where she is."

Doc nodded. That was where she was, in a quarry, floating around lifeless. Doc still didn't want to believe it.

"I didn't mean to do it," he said passionately. "You have to believe me."

Doc didn't answer. He was still reeling from the image of Ella in the water.

"Maybe I'm just crazy," Charlie muttered and looked away.

Doc stared at him. From his experience, "crazy" was just an excuse to do what you wanted. And to get away with it.

"If she would have just shut up," he said. "Nothing would have happened. If she would have just listened to me. I wasn't going to hurt her. That was *never* my intention."

A flicker of anger began to spark inside of Doc again. It was a strong anger and he hadn't been prepared for the force of it as it took over his body. He again told it to settle down but this anger was stronger than the one before. This anger wanted retribution.

"Any man might have done the same thing," Charlie told him.

Any man? Was that what Charlie Patterson was? Any man? What was Doc Muroc? That's when Doc's suspicions were confirmed. Everything became crystal clear. Why they were in the woods, why Charlie had confessed. He'd confessed to get it off his chest. But he knew he wasn't going to do any time for it. He'd never pay for his sins against Ella. But he did want to be absolved of them, as any sinner does.

"You didn't put her in the water," Doc said suddenly. "Did you? We just come out here so you could give me the runaround."

Charlie's head jerked up.

Doc studied him, knowing what this man had planned to do. He knew when they'd stopped to fill a gas can in his trunk what he was going to do with it. He needed it to dispose of the evidence—Doc. It didn't scare him in the least. It was act of desperation but how many other acts of desperation would Charlie Patterson succumb to?

"Where did you put my girl?" he asked.

Charlie didn't answer.

"Where did you put her?" Doc asked. "She's not in the water, is she?"

"No," Charlie said and took a breath. "I have a storage building out behind my house. That's where I put her."

Doc nodded. That's were Ella was, where she'd been all along. This man had put her there. The anger was gone from Doc and he felt calm all of a sudden. He had found peace. He knew what had happened to his child. He knew what he had to do now. And he had to do it fast before Charlie did it to him. It was the survival instinct we all have that carried Doc through this task and he performed it with no doubt that he was doing what he had to do.

Without a word, Doc got up and grabbed the log out of the fire and hit Charlie Patterson across the forehead with it. With one hard whack, the man was on his back. It happened so quickly and without warning that Charlie didn't know what had hit him, or that he'd even been hit.

Doc didn't stare at him, nor did he feel any immediate remorse about what had happened, about what he had done. Did he do the right thing? Was it better to let him live with misery of knowing he was no better than an animal? But the fact was that in the end it would have been either Doc or Charlie. Doc preferred himself.

Charlie fell over with a thump. Doc walked over to him and bludgeoned him until he was sure he was dead. Then, with the calm and reserve he always had, Doc reach inside Charlie's pocket and took out the car keys, picked up Charlie Patterson's body and threw him into the fire. He went all the way back to the car and got the gas can Charlie had intended on using on him. He took it back and poured it onto the fire. He added logs all night and watched him burn.

The fire got hotter and hotter as the night progressed and the smell of burning flesh got fainter and fainter. In the morning, the fire died down and Doc sorted through the ashes for the man's bones, which he crushed with a rock and scattered throughout the woods.

He paused for a moment and wondered if Charlie had done the same thing to Ella. He felt the anger again and kicked at the ground. He prayed that Charlie hadn't lied about where she was.

Once he was done, he went to Charlie's car and got in and drove to his house. It was there, in the storage building, that he was finally reunited with his daughter. He almost broke down when he found her rolled up into a rug. But he held his tears back and did his duty as a father. Her little body was all but gone—she was mostly bones—but it was her. He knew it was her by the shoes poking out from the bottom of the rug. They were the brown alligator shoes that Ruth had commented on.

"Lord, Ella, where did you get those shoes?"

"Like 'em?" she'd asked. "I got them from this store that has used clothes and sells them cheap. Can you believe they only cost ten dollars?"

"You paid ten dollars for those? Used?!"

"Mommy, they're alligator!" Ella had retorted. "Ten dollars is cheap for alligator!"

Ruth had pulled back and, not knowing Doc was listening, said, "You didn't get them from a used clothing store, did you? Did Frank buy them for you?"

"Yeah," Ella said and giggled. "He did."

"Ella," Ruth said. "Don't let a man like that get away."

"I don't plan on it, Mommy," she said.

Doc shook his head and took a deep breath, steeling himself for the task ahead. He didn't look at Ella as he put her into the car and drove all the way back to Cumberland Gap. He didn't take her home, he took her to the woods he'd hunted many times. There, with a shovel he'd taken from the storage building, he dug her grave, giving her back to the Lord and releasing her from this world.

He covered the grave well and found a big rock to mark it. After he was done, he looked around and found a few wild flowers and placed them at the top of the grave. And then he sat down beside it and told Ella he was sorry he'd taken so long to find her. He wouldn't tell anyone that he had found her, not even the police or the FBI. It would be much simpler just to lay her to rest alone. No one need ever know how it had ended for Ella. That was between her and God.

As he sat there, a memory of her came flooding towards him. It was so vivid and real, it was if he were trapped in it. It was her voice, singing so sweetly. Her voice was so young and full of hope and it was clear as a bell. There it was, "*I wouldn't let my dear Savior in...*"

Doc closed his eyes tightly and let the memory envelope him and it made him cry. It was the first time Doc had cried over Ella.

She was sitting in the middle of the bed, singing to the twins when they were toddlers. "*...praise...thhhhheee Lorrrd...I saw the light...*" They cooed at her, watching her face with rapt attention. "*I saw the ligh—ht...*"

It was that Hank Williams' song, *I Saw the Light*, one Doc had sung himself when Ruth made him go to church. Doc had stood in the doorway, unbeknownst to Ella or the twins, and listened as she sang the song. Just before she finished, he quietly stole away.

As he was walking towards his bedroom, he heard a "Daddy?"

He stopped in the girls' room. "What is it, Susie?"

"Ella's sure does have a pretty voice, don't she?"

"Yeah," he said and meant it. He never said anything he didn't mean.

In the years to come, he would visit Ella often. He'd talk to her and tell her things that were going on. He'd tell her how Irene and Susie had gotten married and had babies. He'd tell her how he had once visited baby Olivia in New York City and how proud he was of her. He'd tell her of the twin's shenanigans in the army and but he wouldn't live to tell her of their marriages or children. Doc Muroc would not die from old age, but from the black lung he'd picked up from working so many years in the coal mines.

It's All Over Now

After Doc buried Ella, he drove Charlie Patterson's car back to Knoxville and to Frank Jones's house. It was early morning and Frank was still in bed when he'd heard the banging on his front door. He pulled on his robe and ran downstairs and was relieved when he saw Doc standing there, hat in hand and waiting to tell him something important.

"Hello, Doc," he said and stepped aside. "Come in."

"Don't need to," Doc said. "Boy, I want to tell it's all over now. You move on. Move on with your life. It's time."

"Did you…" Frank began but stopped. "Was she…?"

"Yeah," Doc said. "I done took care of it all. Don't you worry about it now."

Frank stared at him. He understood. It was over. He knew Doc had found Ella but he didn't ask any questions. From the start, Doc had told him he'd find her and he had. It was over and the knowledge of that stabbed Frank in the heart, to know that Ella was really gone. Frank stayed strong and held back his grief. He would break down and he would cry, but he wouldn't do it in front of Doc. He respected him too much for that.

"Doc," Frank said. "I want you to know that I loved her deeply."

"So did I," Doc said and put his hat back on. And then he walked away.

After he took Charlie's car back to his house, Doc boarded the train from Knoxville for the last time. As he rode home, he stared out the window and felt for the first time in a long time a sense of relief.

When he got home, Ruth met him at the door with a smile. "Did you find her?"

She always asked this question and his answer today would be the same as it always was, "No."

Her smile dropped and she sighed, then the smile came back, though less brilliant and she said, "Well, you'll do it next time. Next time you'll find her. Come on in here and let's get you something to eat. You must be starving. I bet you forget to eat, too, didn't you?"

Doc watched her disappear into the kitchen. He almost wanted to tell her but then he knew he couldn't. If she knew how Ella had died, she would have gone crazy. It was best that she never know what had happened or what he had done to Charlie Patterson. Besides that, Ruth had moved on and the news would set her back. She'd given enough of her heart and soul to this. She'd given plenty of herself to her children and Doc wanted her to have some peace for once in her life.

Jean Davis smiled to herself when she heard Charlie Patterson didn't show up for work again. She was told by her ex-coworkers that everyone asked about him but after a few weeks, he was replaced by other gossip. No one would mention him again, not even his own father.

It was all over now. It was time to move on. Doc was relieved; he only wished he could have brought his girl back home to her mother. But that was out of his hands. He knew Ella was in heaven now, watching them from above. The thought comforted him. The pictures he'd taken from Ella's apartment of the baby and her comforted him too. He liked knowing that little Olivia was out there and that meant a piece of Ella was still around and would live forever.

Just after New Years', Doc received a letter from Jean Davis. It read: *"Mr. Muroc, I just wanted to let you know that Ella would be so grateful for what you did. Wherever she is at, she is thanking you. I know I am."*

Doc had to read the letter several times to get what it meant, but then he smiled. That Jean Davis was a good girl and he was glad he'd met her.

Doc folded the paper up and then went to the cook stove and removed one of the eyes. He threw the letter into the fire and watched it burn.

"What was that?" Ruth asked behind him.

"Nothing," he said and replaced the stove eye. "What's for supper?"

Epilogue

Time moved on as it tends to do. During that time, the pieces of the past slowly dissolved into oblivion, leaving the remaining clues as to what really happened out of reach for those of us in the future. We will talk about it, we will think about it, but we never really know what actually happened. All we can do is speculate.

The past remained with everyone and they lived with it. They didn't dissect it nor did they talk about it much after a while. They tried not to think about it or obsess. It was too painful. But Doc had his closure. He had done what any man in his situation would have done.

I never knew my grandfather, but I am sure he was a helluva man. And I am not exactly sure if this is what really happened, but I think it might be.